# RAVEN'S BANE
## TALES OF THE SUNDERING
## TWILIGHT
## DERREN PARSONS

Elven Leaf Publishing

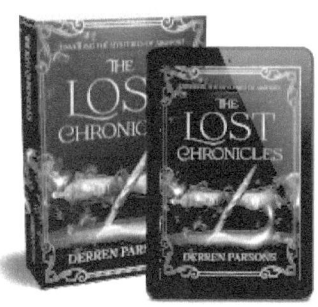

## Your Free Book is Waiting

Join us on a journey through Arghost, a land of ancient wars and enchanting magic. From the icy peaks of Atheron to the arid deserts of the Western Lands, this anthology of riveting tales will transport you to a realm of contrast and wonder.

Meet the voices of elves, dwarves, humans, asakal, and mighty namites as they navigate through the treacherous and beautiful world they inhabit. But be wary, for danger lurks in the form of reptans, wildkin, and other ferocious creatures, waiting to strike from the shadows. Immerse yourself in the magic that weaves through nature and discover the untold stories of Arghost. But beware, for not all mysteries are meant to be revealed...

**Get a free copy of the novella**
***The Lost Chronicles: Unveiling the Mysteries of Arghost.***
www.derrenparsonsauthor.com

# CHAPTER ONE

*The Hunt*

The basket bit into Amara's shoulder as she picked her way through the darkening forest. Moonwort and silverleaf—a simple errand for the elder's stomach remedy that should have been finished an hour ago. The weight of the herbs felt accusatory now, evidence of how long they'd lingered.

'We stayed too long.' Jonah's voice came from ahead, tight with worry.

'The elders can wait for their tea.' Amara tried to sound brave, but her eyes kept finding the shadows between the trees, where the last light couldn't reach. 'Besides, you're the one who insisted on finding the perfect moonwort.'

'Because the last time I brought her crushed leaves, she made me pick them again.' He glanced back with a half-smile that didn't quite reach his eyes. 'In the rain.'

It was a weak joke, but Amara smiled anyway. This was what they did—teased each other, competed over who could spot the rarest herbs, made the work feel less like duty. They'd been doing this together since they were children, back when the baskets were too big for their small hands and everything was an adventure.

That was before the disappearances.

The thought crept in like cold water. Three ravens gone this month. Mara, who taught the fledglings to hunt. Old Corvus, who knew every story of their people. And Elara—sweet Elara, who'd been planning her bonding ceremony for spring.

Gone from the roost when dawn came. Just... gone.

'Amara.' Jonah had stopped walking. 'The warnings—'

'I know.' She did know. The elders had been clear: Never stray far from the village after dark. Never travel alone. Never linger where the trees grow sparse enough for human eyes to find you. The rules had grown stricter with each loss, the old voices growing sharper with fear they tried to mask as wisdom.

The forest had changed with that fear. What was once familiar now felt watchful. Every snap of twig, every rustle of leaves made her heart jump. The other ravens felt it too—you could see it in how they moved through the village, how conversations stopped when someone mentioned the lost ones, how parents kept their children close.

'We should transform,' Jonah said quietly. 'We'd be home in minutes.'

Amara felt the familiar pull of it—that calling that lived in her bones, the knowledge of wings and sky and freedom. To change would be to shed the weight of the basket, the worry, the fear. To become something swift and small and safe in the darkness.

But the elders had forbidden it.

Too many hunters, they said. Too many traps. And if they caught you in the air, if they forced the Wing-Bane down your throat before you could change back...

She shuddered. 'You know we can't. Not until we're closer to the village wards.'

'Then we walk fast.'

They did. The path wound through ancient oaks whose roots had drunk from this earth for centuries before the first raven took wing.

Amara had played among these trees as a child, had learned their names and moods. The grandmother oak with the hollow where she'd hidden during seeking games. The lightning-struck sentinel that marked the halfway point to the herb meadows. The twin maples where she'd kissed Jonah for the first time, three summers ago.

These trees had been her home, her playground, her sanctuary.

Now they felt like a cage.

'Do you think it's true?' Jonah asked suddenly. 'What they're saying about the hunters?'

Amara didn't have to ask what he meant. The whispers had spread through the village like smoke—that the hunters weren't just killing ravens anymore. That they were harvesting them. Taking heads, talons, feathers. Selling them to someone who paid in gold.

'I don't want to think about it.'

'But if it's true—'

'Then we're worth more dead than we ever were alive.' The bitterness in her voice surprised her. 'And there's nothing we can do about it except hide and hope we're not next.'

'We could fight back.'

She stopped walking. 'With what, Jonah? We're not warriors. We gather herbs and weave baskets and tell stories. They have iron and steel and weapons made to kill us.'

'We have wings.'

'Wings they can trap with their cursed flares. Wings they can cage with iron. Wings they can cut from our bodies when we fall.' She was breathing hard now, the fear she'd been pushing down all day rising in her throat like bile. 'My mother says there used to be thousands of us. Now we hide in one village, and even that isn't safe anymore.'

Jonah reached for her hand. His fingers were warm, callused from work. Real. Here. Alive.

'I'm sorry,' he said softly. 'I just... I hate feeling helpless.'

'Me too.'

They stood there in the growing dark, two young ravens who'd been taught to fear the night. Somewhere in the distance, a real raven called—one of the non-shifting kind, the birds their people had been named for. Its cry sounded lonely.

'Come on,' Amara said finally. 'Let's get home.'

They'd taken maybe twenty steps when the sky tore open.

Pale blue light split the darkness like a fallen star—the Earthbind flare, the elders called it. A poacher's curse that choked the change. Amara had heard of it all her life, had listened to the old ones describe it with the same reverence they used for thunderstorms and forest fires: a force of nature, terrible and unstoppable.

She'd never seen one before.

The light was wrong. Too bright, too cold. It cast everything in sharp relief—every leaf, every branch, every shadow suddenly visible in unnatural clarity. The very air seemed to crystallize around it, heavy with magic that tasted of metal and ash on her tongue.

And then came the absence.

She reached for the change instinctively—*wings, feathers, sky*—and found nothing. The calling that had lived in her bones since birth simply... stopped. Like trying to remember a song and finding only silence. Like reaching for a hand that wasn't there.

The Earthbind had trapped them in skin.

'Run.' Jonah's hand clamped on her arm. 'Amara, *run*.'

The basket fell. Herbs scattered across the forest floor—moonwort and silverleaf, gathered with such care, now abandoned. Later, she would remember the waste of it. Later, she would wish that had been the worst thing she lost that night.

Now, she just ran.

Behind them, voices. Human voices, rough and eager.

'That way!'

'Two of them!'

'Don't let them change!'

The forest that had been her home became a nightmare of obstacles. Vines caught at her legs like grasping fingers. Branches lashed her face, drawing blood. Roots rose up to trip her. The blue light painted everything in shades of ice and shadow, turning familiar paths into alien landscape.

Her lungs burned. Sweat slicked her palms. The metallic taste of fear filled her mouth.

*This is how they feel*, she thought with sudden, horrible clarity. *This is how the deer feel when we hunt them. This is how the rabbit feels in the hawk's shadow.*

She'd never understood prey before. Never truly grasped what it meant to be hunted.

She understood now.

'Amara!' Jonah was ahead of her, vaulting a fallen log with the grace of someone who'd spent his whole life learning to move through these woods. 'This way!'

She followed because there was nothing else to do. No wings to carry her up and away. No change to make her small and swift. Just her human body, soft and slow and utterly vulnerable.

The gap between them and their pursuers was closing. She could hear the hunters' breathing now, could hear the heavy thud of boots on earth, could hear the creak of leather and the rattle of steel.

Too close. Much too close to the village.

If they followed Amara and Jonah home, they'd find everyone. The children. The elders. The mothers heavy with eggs. Everyone she'd ever loved, trapped and helpless under the Earthbind's blue glare.

'We can't lead them back,' she gasped.

'I know.' Jonah's face had gone gray, his lips pressed into a thin line. She knew that look—the same expression he wore when he was trying to solve an impossible problem. When he was about to do something brave and stupid.

'Don't—'

'The blast,' he cut her off. 'It's trapped us. We won't outrun them like this.'

He was right. They both knew it. In raven form, they could have been home in heartbeats. As humans, weighed down by flesh and fear, they were painfully slow.

The voices behind them grew louder. Closer.

'There! I see movement!'

'Cut them off at the ravine!'

They burst into a small clearing, moonlight breaking through the canopy in pale shafts. Jonah stumbled to a halt, spinning to scan their surroundings. His eyes locked on something ahead—a massive fallen oak, its trunk hollow with rot.

'There.' He grabbed her hand, pulled her forward. 'Hide in the log.'

'No.' The word came out fierce. 'We stay together.'

'If we both hide, they'll find us. But if I draw them off—'

'They'll kill you!'

'Maybe.' His hand tightened on hers. 'Or maybe I'll lose them in the dark. You know I'm faster.'

It was true. Jonah had always been quicker on foot, more agile in the trees. Even as children playing chase, he'd always won their races.

But this wasn't a game.

'I can't—' Her voice broke. 'Jonah, please.'

'Listen to me.' He cupped her face with both hands, forcing her to meet his eyes. They were dark in the strange light, but she could see the fear in them. The determination. 'If we both die here, who warns the village? Who tells them the hunters are using Earthbind? Who tells them they're this close to finding us?'

'You tell them. You run. I'll hide and—'

'You're a terrible liar, Amara. You always have been.' He smiled, sad and crooked. 'But you're the bravest person I know. You can do this.'

'Don't.' Tears blurred her vision. This felt like goodbye. This felt like the last time.

'I'll come back,' he promised. 'I'll lose them in the woods and circle around. You wait here until it's safe, then you go straight home. Tell the elders everything. Make them listen.'

He was already backing away, toward the sound of approaching boots.

'Stay safe,' she whispered.

'Always am.'

He flashed her one last smile—bright and false and heartbreaking—then turned and ran, crashing through the undergrowth with enough noise to wake the dead.

Making sure they heard him. Making sure they followed.

The hunters' voices shifted direction, moving away from her hiding place. Chasing Jonah into the dark.

Amara crawled into the hollow log on hands and knees, rot and ancient wood closing around her like a coffin. The smell of decay filled her nose. Beetles scattered from her intrusion. Somewhere in the darkness, a spider crawled across her hand.

She barely noticed.

All she could hear was Jonah's footsteps, growing fainter. All she could feel was the horrible, crushing weight of being still while he ran toward danger.

*Please,* she prayed to gods she'd never quite believed in. *Please let him be fast enough. Smart enough. Lucky enough.*

*Please don't let me lose him.*

The hollow log was cramped and dark and smelled of death. Not the clean death of a fallen tree returning to earth, but something older. Something that reminded Amara of the rabbit she'd found when she was seven—the one that had crawled into a hollow to die, its body slowly becoming part of the wood.

She pressed herself against the rotting bark and tried to breathe quietly.

Voices drifted through the forest. The hunters, arguing.

'Lost him at the creek.'

'Damned bird-spawn moves like smoke.'

'Should've brought more men. Two aren't enough for this.'

*Two.* Just two hunters, and they'd nearly caught both of them. What chance did any raven have if a whole group came? What chance did the village have?

'The other one's around here somewhere,' a different voice said. Rougher. Meaner. 'Girl, by the size of her. Probably hiding.'

Footsteps. Coming closer.

Amara's heart hammered so hard she was certain they'd hear it. She drew her knees up to her chest, making herself as small as possible in the hollow's darkness. A childhood hiding place, returned to her now. Once, she and Jonah had played seeking games in logs like this, laughing when the finder gave up too soon.

This wasn't a game.

The footsteps stopped. Close. Too close.

'Check that log, Garik.'

A pause. Then: 'It's probably empty.'

'Since when do you waste time probably? Check it.'

Silence stretched. Amara could hear her own blood rushing in her ears. Could feel sweat trickling down her spine despite the night's chill.

Then the footsteps moved away.

'Nothing here. Let's keep moving.'

Relief flooded through her so intensely it made her dizzy. He'd lied. The one called Garik had looked at her hiding place and lied to his companion.

But why?

She didn't have time to puzzle over it. The voices were fading, moving deeper into the forest. Following Jonah's trail.

*Stay hidden*, he'd told her. *Wait until it's safe.*

But how long was safe? How would she know when to move?

She waited. Counted her heartbeats. Tried to slow her breathing. The forest gradually quieted around her. An owl called in the distance—a real owl, not one of the shape-shifters who sometimes wore that form. The wind picked up, rustling leaves.

Normal sounds. Safe sounds.

Amara uncurled slowly, muscles cramping from the stillness. She needed to move. Needed to get home, to warn the elders, to do what Jonah had asked.

She was halfway out of the log when she heard them coming back.

Different this time. Triumphant.

'Good weight on this one,' a voice said. 'The magikas will pay well.'

'Long as the head's intact, he don't care about the rest.'

'Still say we should've caught both. Double the coin.'

'The girl's probably halfway home by now, spreading panic. Makes the next hunt harder.'

Amara froze, one leg out of the log, the other still trapped inside. She couldn't see them yet, but they were close. Getting closer.

And they were talking about Jonah like he was already dead.

*No. No, no, no.*

She saw them before they saw her—two men emerging from the trees, one tall and lean, the other shorter and broader. The shorter one carried something that gleamed pale in the moonlight.

For a heartbeat, she didn't understand what she was seeing.

Then the world tilted sideways.

A raven's head swung from the hunter's belt, its black feathers matted with drying blood. The beak had been cut cleanly at the base, leaving a raw stump of bone and flesh. The eyes were half-closed, filmy with death.

But she knew those eyes. Knew the slight crook in that beak, broken when they were children and never quite healed straight. Knew the pattern of those feathers—darker on the left side, where a childhood accident had scarred the skin beneath.

*Jonah.*

The sound that came from her throat wasn't quite human. It was the cry of a raven, trapped in the wrong body. Grief and rage and horror all compressed into a single, anguished note.

The hunters spun toward her.

'There!'

She was running before conscious thought caught up. Running blind, branches tearing at her clothes, her face, her hands. Behind her, shouts and crashing pursuit.

But she didn't care about being caught anymore.

Didn't care about being quiet, being careful, being safe.

Jonah was dead. They'd killed him. Cut off his head like a trophy, like he was an animal, like his life meant nothing more than the weight of gold it could buy.

The Earthbind's blue glow had faded at some point—she couldn't remember when. The magic released its grip on her bones.

And the change came roaring back.

She'd transformed a hundred times before. A thousand. It was as natural as breathing, as automatic as her heart beating. But this was different.

This was fury.

Her bones hollowed and reformed. Flesh compressed, restructured. Arms became wings, legs folded into talons. Her vision sharpened, colors shifting into the spectrum only ravens could see. Feathers burst from her skin in a rush of painful, perfect metamorphosis.

Her clothes fell away like shed bark.

She launched from the ground with a power she'd never felt before, wings catching air with a snap that echoed through the trees. Up, up into the canopy, into the safety of branches and leaves and sky.

Below, the hunters shouted in confusion and dismay.

'It changed!'

'Grab the nets!'

'Too late, it's gone!'

She should have flown away. Should have raced home to warn the village, to tell them what had happened, to break her mother's heart with the news of Jonah's death.

Instead, she perched in the high branches and looked down.

Looked down and saw them.

Two men in hunter's leather, weapons at their belts, Jonah's severed head still swinging from the shorter one's belt like a grotesque prize. They were searching the ground where she'd dropped her clothes, arguing about which direction she'd flown.

She watched them. Memorized them.

The tall one had a scar across his jaw. The shorter one wore a ring on his left hand that caught the moonlight. They moved with the confidence of men who'd done this before. Who would do it again.

They'd killed Jonah for gold. Had ended his life without hesitation, without mercy, without even knowing his name.

And they were hunting for more.

Rage settled into something colder. Harder. A determination that felt like ice in her veins.

*Remember them,* she told herself. *Remember their faces. Remember what they did.*

The tall one—the one who'd been called Garik, the one who'd lied about checking her hiding place—pulled out a flask and took a long drink. Even from this distance, she could smell the alcohol. Could see the slight slump of his shoulders.

He looked... tired. Almost sad.

But he'd still hunted Jonah. Still been there when the knife fell.

'Let's head back,' he said. 'We're done here.'

'Should hunt the girl—'

'I said we're done.' There was an edge to his voice. Authority. The other man subsided with a grunt of annoyance.

They turned and walked away, Jonah's head bouncing against the shorter man's hip with every step.

Amara stayed in the tree until they were gone. Until the forest grew quiet again. Until the moon had moved a hand's width across the sky.

Then she flew.

Not toward home. Not yet.

She followed them.

Stayed high in the canopy, moving from tree to tree in absolute silence. Ravens were hunters too—she knew how to move without being seen, how to track without being heard. These skills, learned in pursuit of rabbits and mice, turned now toward darker prey.

The hunters emerged from the forest into farmland. Fields stretched silver under the moon, and beyond them, the yellow glow of the town. Amara had never been this close to a human settlement before. Had never wanted to be.

She watched the hunters approach a building on the town's edge—larger than the others, with light spilling from its windows and the sound of voices and laughter pouring into the night.

The shorter man went inside immediately, still carrying his prize.

But Garik—the tall one, the one who'd lied—stopped at the door. Stood there for a long moment, staring at his hands in the lantern light.

Even from a distance, even through her rage and grief, Amara could see his expression.

He looked like a man who'd just woken from a nightmare to find it was real.

Then he shook his head, straightened his shoulders, and went inside.

The door closed behind him, and Amara was alone in the darkness with her grief and her fury and the terrible knowledge of what she'd lost.

Somewhere in that building, they would celebrate. Would drink and laugh and count their gold. Would talk about Jonah like he was nothing more than a successful hunt.

And tomorrow, they would do it again.

Would hunt another raven. Take another head. End another life.

Unless someone stopped them.

Amara spread her wings and flew toward home, a plan already forming in her mind. A plan that was probably foolish. Definitely dangerous.

But Jonah had died to save her. Had run into the darkness so she could escape.

She wouldn't let that sacrifice mean nothing.

The hunters thought they were predators. Thought the ravens were helpless prey, fit only for harvesting.

They were about to learn they were wrong.

# CHAPTER TWO

*The Weight of Gold*

G ARIK

The tavern was loud enough to drown thought, which was exactly what Garik wanted.

He drained the last of his ale and wiped his mouth on his sleeve. The heat from the fire seeped into his bones, but it did nothing for the cold that had settled in his chest. The warmth he felt came from the chase, from the kill, from the weight of gold that would soon line his pockets.

It should have felt good. It used to feel good.

Across the table, Ragar wore the same look he always did after a successful hunt—eyes bright, jaw loose with drink and satisfaction. Pride. That's what it was. Pride in a job well done.

Garik couldn't remember the last time he'd felt that.

'Another,' he said, lifting his empty cup.

Ragar grinned and stood, chair scraping against the worn wooden floor as he pushed into the crowd. The tavern was packed tonight—farmers celebrating a good harvest, merchants passing through, other hunters trading stories of their latest kills.

Garik leaned back and let the noise wash over him. Drunks laughed too loudly. A bard butchered a tune near the hearth, but no one seemed to care. The air stank of smoke and sweat and old beer—a smell he'd known all his life, as familiar as his own skin.

They'd done well tonight. Too well, maybe.

That was the trouble.

*Don't take more than needed.*

His father's voice, echoing from a decade ago. Lessons taught in this very forest, before age and injury had forced the old man to give up the hunting life.

*The woods provide, but only if you don't get greedy. Take what you need. Leave the rest. That's how you ensure there's always something to come back to.*

Good advice. Wise advice.

Advice Garik had been ignoring more and more lately.

'Good hunt, Garik.'

A man had stopped beside the table. Callum. Old, weathered, one of the better trackers before his knees gave out. He leaned heavily on a cane now, but his eyes were still sharp.

'Aye,' Garik said, because what else was there to say?

'Leave some for the rest of us next time.' Callum smiled, but there was something in it that wasn't quite humor. A warning, maybe. Or a judgment.

Garik watched him go, unease tightening in his gut.

How many had they taken this month? Five? Six? He'd lost count. And that was just him and Ragar. The other hunters were bringing in numbers too. The whole town was flush with raven-coin, the hunters buying rounds at the tavern, the merchants raising prices because they knew people could pay.

It couldn't last. Even Garik, who'd never been particularly clever with numbers or planning, could see that.

But Ragar had other ideas.

He returned and set two full tankards down with a heavy thunk, sloshing foam over the rims.

'Jian was talking,' Ragar said, lowering his voice even though the tavern's din would drown any eavesdroppers. 'There's a magika out west. Volthar. Pays well for raven spoils.'

Garik stiffened. 'How well?'

Ragar shrugged. 'Enough to make this worth repeating. Triple what we're getting from the usual buyers. Maybe more.'

Triple. The word hung in the air between them like bait on a hook.

Garik stared into his cup. Too many birds. Too much coin. That was how men like him lost their way. He'd seen it before—hunters who got greedy, who took too much, who ended up with nothing because they'd killed everything worth hunting.

But triple.

He had debts. His sister's husband had died last winter, leaving her with three children and no way to feed them. The roof on his own cottage leaked, and he'd been putting off repairs for two years.

Triple would solve all of that.

All it would cost was more ravens.

*They're not just birds,* a voice whispered in the back of his mind. The same voice that had made him lie at the hollow log, that had stopped him from dragging the girl out of her hiding place.

He pushed it away.

'If he wants more,' Garik said at last, 'we'll see.'

Ragar grinned. 'That's the spirit.'

Was it? Garik wasn't sure anymore.

He'd started hunting ravens when he was sixteen—an age when boys became men by proving they could provide. His father had been too injured to teach him everything, so he'd learned from the other hunters. Learned to read the signs of raven presence. Learned to set snares that wouldn't be detected. Learned that Earthbind flares, expensive as they were, could trap a shifting raven in human form long enough to catch it.

Learned to think of them as *it*, not *them*. As *ravens*, not *people*.

Because if you started thinking of them as people, you couldn't do the job. Couldn't bring yourself to spring the trap, to draw the knife, to take the head that Volthar and his kind paid so well for.

The other hunters said ravens weren't really human. Just wore human shape, the way a wolf wore sheep's clothing. They were animals underneath, no matter what form they took. Killing them was no different than killing deer or rabbit.

Garik had believed that once.

Now...

Now he remembered the way the male raven had looked at him in the forest. The intelligence in those eyes. The fear.

Now he wondered if he'd been lying to himself for eight years.

'Garik?' Ragar was watching him with narrowed eyes. 'You alright?'

'Fine.' He took a long drink, letting the ale burn its way down his throat. 'Just tired.'

'We made good coin tonight. You should be celebrating.'

Should be. But the weight in his pocket felt heavier than gold had any right to feel.

Around them, the tavern roared on. Someone started a drinking song, bawdy and loud. The bard gave up trying to compete and joined in instead. Ragar turned to shout something at a friend across the room.

Garik sat in the noise and the warmth and the golden glow of success, and felt absolutely nothing.

No—not nothing.

Guilt.

It had been creeping up on him for months now. A slow poison, getting worse with every hunt. Tonight, it had finally bloomed into something he couldn't ignore.

He kept seeing her face. The girl in the forest. Young—maybe seventeen or eighteen. Too young to die. She'd looked at Ragar's belt, at what hung there, and the sound she'd made...

*That wasn't the cry of an animal.*

He drained his tankard in three long swallows.

Tomorrow, he'd go back to the forest. Tomorrow, he'd set new snares and check old ones. Tomorrow, he'd hunt ravens because that's what he did, what he'd always done, what he needed to do to survive.

But tonight, he let himself wonder if survival was worth the cost.

And hated himself for even asking the question.

The cottage was dark when Garik finally stumbled home, the last of the ale making his steps unsteady. He fumbled with the latch, cursing under his breath when it stuck.

The door swung open to reveal a single candle burning on the table.

Leira sat beside it, still dressed despite the late hour. Sixteen years old and already carrying herself like someone twice that age—straight-backed, serious, her dark hair pulled back in a practical braid. She had her mother's features, the same sharp cheekbones and dark eyes that had once looked at him with love instead of judgment.

Her mother had died bringing her into the world. Sometimes Garik wondered if that was punishment for what he'd become.

'You're awake,' he said, the words coming out slurred. He winced at the sound of his own voice.

'Someone has to make sure you don't fall in the fire.' Her tone was flat, empty of the warmth she'd shown him as a child. When she used to wait up for him like this, it had been excitement, not duty. *Papa's home!* she'd cry, running to throw her arms around his legs.

Now she didn't move from her chair.

Garik set his hunting pack down carefully, trying not to let it thud too heavily against the floor. Trying not to think about what stained the leather. 'You should be sleeping. You have work in the morning.'

'So do you.' She stood, moving to the hearth where a pot of stew sat cooling. She ladled some into a bowl with mechanical efficiency. 'Mrs. Harrow sent this over. Said you looked thin.'

'I'm fine.'

'You're drunk.'

He couldn't argue with that. He sank into his chair, the wood creaking under his weight. The cottage felt smaller with both of them in it, the silence between them taking up more space than their bodies.

Leira set the bowl in front of him without meeting his eyes.

'Thank you,' he said quietly.

She didn't respond. Just returned to her seat and picked up the shirt she'd been mending, her needle moving with sharp, angry precision.

Garik stared at the stew. His stomach turned at the thought of eating, but he forced himself to take a bite. Mrs. Harrow was a good woman, widowed young, who'd helped raise Leira when Garik had been too lost in grief and guilt to be a proper father. The least he could do was eat her food.

The silence stretched.

'There was a girl,' Garik heard himself say. The ale was making him stupid, loosening his tongue. 'In the forest tonight. Young. Your age, maybe.'

Leira's hands stilled on the fabric.

'She got away,' he continued, not sure why he was telling her this. 'I let her hide. Didn't tell Ragar.'

'Do you want me to thank you?' Her voice was cold. 'For showing basic human decency? For not murdering a child?'

The words hit like a slap. 'Leira—'

'No.' She set down the mending with careful control, but he could see her hands shaking. 'No, you don't get to do this. You don't get to come home drunk and tell me about the one you *didn't* kill, as if that makes the others disappear.'

'I'm trying to provide for us. To give you a life—'

'I don't want this life!' Her voice cracked, the composure breaking. 'I don't want a life built on blood money. I don't want to wake up every morning wondering if today's the day someone comes to arrest you, or worse—if you don't come home at all because one of them fought back.'

'The ravens don't fight back.'

'They should.' She stood abruptly, the chair scraping against the floor. 'Maybe if they did, you'd finally see them as something more than coin on wings.'

Garik stood too, swaying slightly. 'You think I like this? You think I enjoy—'

'I think you've convinced yourself you don't have a choice.' Leira's eyes were bright with unshed tears, but her voice remained steady. 'That's what frightens me most. You've told yourself this lie so many times you actually believe it.'

'It's not a lie. We need—'

'We need food and shelter. Not gold. Not blood money from selling *people's heads* to magikas.' She spat the words like poison. 'Mrs. Harrow offered me work at the bakery. I could apprentice there. Learn a trade. We could survive on that.'

'Barely.'

'But we'd survive clean.' She crossed her arms, a defensive gesture that made her look younger. Vulnerable. 'My mother died so I could live, Papa. Don't make that meaningless by teaching me that survival justifies anything.'

The mention of her mother hit him like a physical blow. He sank back into his chair, all the fight draining out of him.

'Your mother would be ashamed of me,' he said quietly.

'Yes.' Leira didn't soften the word. Didn't offer false comfort. 'She would be. But she'd also believe you could change. That's the difference between her and me.'

'You don't think I can change?'

'I don't know anymore.' She picked up the candle, its light casting harsh shadows across her young face. 'I used to believe in you. Used to think you were the bravest, strongest man in the world. Now I just... I don't know who you are.'

She walked toward her small sleeping alcove, pausing at the curtain that divided it from the main room.

'The girl you let live tonight,' she said without turning around. 'She has a father somewhere. A mother. People who love her and are probably sick with worry right now, wondering if she'll come home.'

'I know.'

'Do you?' Now she did turn, and the look in her eyes made him feel smaller than he'd ever felt. 'Because the boy you killed—he had people too. And they're not wondering anymore. They know. They're burying him. Mourning him. Hating you.'

'Leira—'

'I'm glad you let the girl live, Papa. I am. But one act of mercy doesn't erase eight years of murder.' She let the curtain fall, her voice muffled now but still clear. 'Good night.'

'Leira, wait—' Garik stood, the chair scraping loudly against the floor.

She emerged from behind the curtain, her face set. 'What?'

'I...' He reached for her, trying to find words that might bridge the chasm between them. 'I'm trying. You have to understand, I'm—'

'Trying?' Her voice rose. 'You're going back tomorrow, aren't you? Back to the forest. Back to hunting them.'

The silence was answer enough.

'That's what I thought.' She turned away.

Frustration boiled over. Garik grabbed her shoulder—harder than he meant to, 'Don't walk away from me. I'm still your father. I'm doing this for us, for you—'

'Let go.' Her voice was very quiet. Very controlled.

He realized what he'd done—the pressure of his grip, the flash of fear in her eyes—and released her immediately, stumbling back. 'Leira, I didn't mean—'

But she was already moving.

'Where are you going?' Garik demanded, his voice rough with shame and anger and desperation. 'It's late. It's not safe.'

'Safer than here.' She yanked open the door.

'Leira!'

She paused in the doorway, her back to him. 'When you figure out who you want to be—the father I used to know, or the hunter who kills children for gold—you let me know.'

Then she was gone, the door slamming behind her hard enough to rattle the dishes on the table.

Garik stood frozen in the empty cottage, staring at the closed door. His hand still tingled where he'd grabbed her. He could feel the ghost of her shoulder under his fingers, could see the way she'd flinched.

*Just like her mother used to flinch, toward the end.*

No. He wasn't that man. He wasn't violent. He didn't hurt the people he loved.

But his fingers had left marks before. He'd told himself it was an accident, that he'd only meant to keep her from leaving, that she'd pulled away too hard and made it worse.

More lies.

He sank back into his chair, buried his face in his hands, and for the first time in years, let himself cry.

Outside, in the dark streets of Wyntown, his daughter walked toward the river with tears streaming down her face and a fresh bruise forming on her shoulder.

# CHAPTER THREE

*Choices*

The gathering had already turned ugly by the time Caelen reached the square.

Voices clashed beneath the ancient roost-trees, their branches heavy with the weight of generations. Grief bled into anger, raw and jagged. Jonah's name passed from mouth to mouth like a wound pressed too often, each repetition making it bleed fresh.

Caelen pushed through the crowd, fists clenched so tight his nails bit into his palms. His jaw ached from clenching. Jonah had taught him to listen to the forest, to read its silences as carefully as its sounds. Had been steady when Caelen was reckless, patient when Caelen raged.

Gone now. Cut down like timber.

Near the ceremonial fire, Amara stood surrounded by women offering empty comfort. She accepted their murmured condolences without moving, without blinking, her body rigid as carved wood. When someone said Jonah's name too loudly, her shoulders jerked—a flinch she couldn't hide—then she went still again, arms wrapped tight around her ribs as if physically holding herself together. Her eyes stayed fixed on the flames, seeing nothing. Or seeing too much.

Caelen looked away. The ache in his chest sharpened, spreading like poison through his veins.

A young hunter near the front—Daven, barely old enough to fly alone—hurled a pebble into the fire. Sparks exploded upward in an angry shower. Someone hissed in warning, but the boy's voice cracked through the noise: 'They took him like an animal.'

The words hung in the air, horrible in their truth.

'Enough!' Tarron's voice cut through the chaos like an axe through wood.

The baker stood with his flour-dusted apron still tied, hands balled at his sides, his weathered face harder than Caelen had ever seen it. Tarron, who'd never raised his voice above a gentle chiding, who hummed while he kneaded dough, who always had a sweet roll for the children—Tarron looked ready to kill.

It startled the crowd into ragged stillness.

'We keep burying our dead,' Tarron said, each word deliberate. 'And we do nothing. That ends now.'

Murmurs rippled outward through the gathering—some agreement, some fear, some both tangled together.

Vulred stepped forward, his walking staff thumping against the packed earth with the weight of authority. His shoulders sagged beneath age and grief, but his eyes burned with a fire Caelen recognized. The same fire that lived in his own chest, hot and demanding.

'We fight,' Vulred said. The words were simple, but they carried decades of loss. 'Like we should have years ago.'

Caelen felt heat rise in his chest, his heart hammering against his ribs. He moved closer to the fire, drawn by the promise of action after so much helplessness.

'Maybe we don't fight alone,' he said, loud enough to carry. Heads turned. 'Maybe we ask the Fae for aid.'

The name drew a sharp, collective intake of breath. The old tales spoke of Fae bargains, sharp as thorns but binding as blood oaths.

Jonah had laughed at them once, called them children's stories meant to frighten fledglings into obedience. Now Caelen wondered if laughter was a luxury they could no longer afford.

Luthais snorted from his place near the elder's circle, thick arms crossed over his butcher's apron, still dark with the morning's work. 'The Fae?' His voice dripped skepticism. 'They guard their trees, not the Arvi. They'd as soon watch us die as lift a finger to help.'

'Then we make them care,' Caelen shot back. 'We remind them that we're part of this forest too. That our blood feeds the same earth as their precious oaks.'

'The boy speaks madness,' someone muttered.

'The boy speaks truth,' another voice countered.

Illdran raised one weathered hand, and the crowd quieted—though fists stayed clenched and eyes kept darting toward the shadowed trees beyond the square, as if expecting hunters to step out of the darkness at any moment.

'The Fae protect the forest,' Illdran said, his voice carrying the weight of his years. 'That is their charge, their sacred duty. Ours is to endure. To survive. To outlast our enemies through patience and caution.'

Caelen shook his head, frustration boiling over. 'The forest is our home too. We nest in these trees. We hunt in these woods. We die defending them. How is that not worthy of their aid?'

Illdran looked at him then, truly looked. The firelight carved deep shadows in the lines of his face, making him seem older than the ancient oaks themselves.

'You are young,' he said, not unkindly. 'You see only the fire in front of you, feel only the rage of fresh grief. But I have lived through three generations of our people. I have seen what happens when we act in anger. We need allies, not enemies. We reach out carefully. We wait for the right moment.'

'Waiting.' The word came out bitter on Caelen's tongue. 'Again.'

His voice carried farther than he intended, bouncing off the trees and back. 'Our clan is dying. How many more vanish before waiting becomes extinction? How many more heads do they take before there's no one left to mourn?'

A low growl of agreement rose from the back of the crowd. Someone kicked dirt toward the fire in frustration. Amara's head lifted slightly at the word 'extinction,' her hollow eyes focusing for just a moment before the weight of her grief pulled them down again.

Illdran's expression hardened into something implacable, ancient as stone. 'Enough.'

The single word fell like a judge's hammer.

Silence followed. Heavy. Unforgiving. Absolute.

The elder held Caelen's gaze for a long moment, and Caelen saw it clearly—the decision had already been made. Had been made before the gathering even began. This was performance, not discussion. A show of considering options they'd already discarded.

Illdran turned away first, addressing the crowd with finality. 'No one leaves the village alone. Not now. Not after this. We double the watch on the perimeter. We stay within the wards. We wait for the hunters' attention to move elsewhere.'

The meeting dissolved into angry whispers, shoulders brushing roughly as people turned away. Someone muttered 'coward' under their breath—Caelen couldn't tell who, but the sentiment echoed in his own heart. A woman near Amara reached to touch her arm in comfort. Amara stepped back without a word, her face blank as winter sky, and disappeared into the press of bodies like smoke dissolving into air.

Caelen stepped back from the fire, pulse roaring in his ears, drowning out the continued arguments around him. He knew that tone Illdran had used. Had heard it before, after Mara disappeared. After old Corvus never returned from a morning flight. After Elara vanished on the eve of her bonding ceremony.

The tone that meant: *We will do nothing, and you will accept it.*

He left before anyone could stop him, before the rage building in his chest could spill out in words he couldn't take back.

Caelen kept moving until the forest thinned and the road emerged between the trees, a scar of packed earth cutting through green shadow.

Morning dew soaked through his boots, cold clinging to his calves like grasping hands. He slowed only when the packed earth replaced leaf-mold and root, when the ancient trees gave way to younger growth that didn't know his name.

The road lay quiet save for the occasional creak of passing carts—traders and farmers rolling between Silenthollow and Wyntown like insects crawling the spine of the forest, oblivious to the grief rotting in the trees around them.

A cart approached from the east, its wheels cutting deep grooves in the mud.

Caelen stepped aside and raised a hand in greeting. 'Excuse me. You heading to Wyntown?'

The driver reined in his horse and looked Caelen over with the wary assessment of someone who'd lived long enough to know danger wore many faces. Old. Weathered. Bent forward as if the road itself had shaped him over decades of travel.

'Aye,' the man said. His voice was rough as tree bark. 'What's it to ya?'

'Mind if I ride with you? I can pay.' Caelen didn't have coin, but humans responded to the promise of it.

The man frowned, eyes narrowing. Caelen held his gaze, schooling his features into something open and harmless. Distrust came easily between their kinds. Trust did not. But this was not the time for pride.

The man snorted. 'Keep your coin. Don't see why not.' Then, suspicion creeping back: 'Strange place to be walking alone, though. What were you doing out here?'

Caelen climbed onto the cart, the wood creaking under his weight. He settled himself on a barrel, careful to keep his shadow close. 'Hunting,' he said. 'Heard something in the woods. Didn't like the sound of it.'

The man's eyes narrowed further. 'In there?' He jerked his chin toward the forest they'd left behind.

Caelen nodded. 'Trees were groaning. Like something was wrong. Like they were in pain.'

'Don't linger in those woods,' the man said, his voice dropping to something almost reverent. Almost fearful. 'They remember things. Old things. Things best left alone.'

Caelen shrugged, playing the part of the foolish young hunter. 'Elk are fat this season. Seemed worth checking.'

The man laughed once, sharp and humorless. 'Fat ain't worth dying for, boy.'

'Figured that out quick enough.'

'Where's your gear then? Your bow? Your knife?'

'Dropped it when I ran.' Caelen met the man's eyes steadily. 'Wasn't going to stop for a bow when something big was moving through the brush toward me.'

The man grunted, apparently satisfied with this show of self-preservation, and clicked his tongue. The horse leaned into the traces, and the cart lurched forward, wheels finding their rhythm on the rutted road.

They rode in silence for a while. The cart rattled over stones and roots. The smell of horse sweat and old leather filled the air, mixing with the scent of whatever goods the man was hauling—grain, maybe, or dried herbs. Caelen kept his eyes on the road ahead, counting his breaths, keeping his heartbeat steady.

'Don't recognize you,' the man said at last, breaking the silence. 'Where you from?'

Caelen had prepared for this. 'Traveling with my father. We're merchants—furs and amber, mostly. Out of Amberguard, by way of Alesia.'

The man nodded as if that explained everything, as if the wide world were full of young men wandering roads alone. 'Long way from home. Never been to Alesia myself.' He spat over the side of the cart. 'Best advice I can give you, lad? Stay out of those woods. Whatever you heard in there, whatever you think you saw—forget it. Some things, you let them be.'

Caelen glanced at the trees sliding past, their familiar shapes and shadows calling to something deep in his bones. His forest. His home. Now a place he had to sneak away from like a thief.

'Aye,' he said quietly. 'I will.'

The bridge came into view as the road dipped down toward the river valley. Bearwater Bridge arched over the water, its stone darkened by age and constant damp, slick with moss on the shadowed side. Beyond it, Wyntown spread across the hills like a scab, roofs clustered along the water's edge in haphazard rows. Smoke rose in thin lines from a hundred chimneys. The mountains stood beyond it all, distant and pale with early snow that would deepen as winter came.

The cart slowed as they approached the bridge.

Caelen jumped down before the driver could think better of his generosity. 'Thank you for the ride.'

The man lifted a hand in acknowledgment and drove on, his cart disappearing into the flow of traffic crossing the bridge.

Caelen paused at the bridge's edge and looked back once. The forest pressed close on the far bank, dark and patient, waiting for him to return. Or waiting to swallow him whole. He couldn't tell which.

Then he turned and crossed, the sound of the river swallowed by voices and trade and the constant din of human life.

Wyntown closed around him like a fist.

Mud sucked at Caelen's boots with each step, the street churned to a thick soup by constant traffic. Carts crowded the narrow road, their wheels carving deep ruts through the ground. Traders argued about prices in voices that carried over the general chaos. Children ran laughing through puddles, spraying filth up their legs, oblivious to the dirt or the cold or the danger of being trampled.

Life carried on here, loud and careless. Heedless of the grief rotting in the forest. Heedless of Jonah's blood still staining the leaves.

Caelen kept his head down and moved with the flow of bodies, just another traveler in a town that saw dozens every day.

But he watched his shadow as he walked.

In the flat morning light, it refused to behave properly. It thinned and tapered at the edges, pulling into angles no man's shadow should hold. Too long in places. Too narrow in others. A hint of something wing-like where there should have been a shoulder, a suggestion of talons where his feet touched the ground.

Cloud cover helped. Without direct sun, the shape blurred, passed for nothing more than a trick of light and movement. Still, he stayed close to walls and carts, where shadows tangled and broke apart, where his wrongness could hide among other wrongness.

One glance held too long would be enough to damn him.

He found the tavern by following the noise—raucous laughter and raised voices spilling into the street like poisoned water.

Inside, heat and stink pressed close, making him want to gag. Sweat. Ale gone sour in unwashed cups. Too many bodies packed together in too little space. He forced himself forward, ignoring the way his stomach tightened at the smell, the way his skin crawled at the proximity of so many humans.

'What'll it be?' The barkeep barely looked up, wiping a cup with a rag that looked dirtier than the vessel.

'Ale,' Caelen answered, keeping his voice even, unremarkable.

The mug was thrust into his hand with the expectation of payment. He counted out the coins carefully—too much hesitation would mark him as foreign, too little as a fool. The barkeep grunted and turned away.

Caelen swallowed and kept his face still as the bitterness hit. Warm. Flat. Barely alcoholic. He wiped his mouth and nodded as if it pleased him, as if he'd tasted worse and been grateful for it.

He chose a seat where the light was bad and the floor uneven, where he could press his back to the wall and watch the room. And listen.

Farmers complained about the weather. About soil that wouldn't yield. About taxes that bled them dry. Names drifted through the noise like leaves on a current—merchants, local nobles, women mar-

ried or courted or spurned. The mundane concerns of people who
didn't know they were being hunted.

Then—

'They say Volthar's building something out west.'

Caelen's hand stilled on his cup. He didn't turn his head, didn't
show any sign of interest. But every sense focused on the conversation
happening two tables away.

'An army?' The second voice sounded skeptical.

'That's what I heard. Soldiers, weapons, something big.'

'Rubbish. Volthar's a magika, not a warlord. Probably just expand-
ing his estate, and rumors turned it into an invasion force.'

Nervous laughter followed, but it sounded forced. The talk shifted
to safer topics—crop yields, a merchant's daughter who'd run off
with a soldier, the price of iron—but the name stayed with Caelen,
heavy as stone in his gut.

Volthar. A magika building something.

Movement behind him made him tense, but he forced himself to
remain still.

Two men sat at the table directly to his left, close enough that he
could smell the leather of their hunting gear, the metallic tang of old
blood not quite washed away. He didn't need to look to know what
they were.

But he did look. Carefully. A glance that seemed accidental, unin-
terested.

Garik and Ragar. The names came to him from Amara's descrip-
tion. The tall one with the scar. The shorter, broader one.

The hunters who'd killed Jonah.

Caelen's fingers tightened around his mug until his knuckles went
white. He forced himself to breathe, to stay seated, to not reach for
the knife hidden beneath his coat.

'Crowded for this early,' Garik said. His voice was rough, tired.

'Farmers drink before work,' Ragar replied with a shrug. 'Makes the day easier. Makes everything easier.'

Garik didn't laugh. 'I can't keep doing this.'

A pause. Caelen could feel the weight of it.

'Leira again?' Ragar's tone suggested this was an old argument.

'She won't even look at me anymore. Won't sit at the table when I'm home. Spends all her time at the neighbor's, helping with their children, anything to avoid being in the same room.'

'She's sixteen. All girls that age hate their fathers.'

'It's not that.' Garik's voice dropped lower. 'She knows what we do. Knows what I bring home. Last week I came back and found her crying in the kitchen. Wouldn't tell me why, but I saw her looking at my gear. At the blood on my coat.'

'She'll come around when she realizes the coin buys her food.'

'She said she'd rather starve.'

A pause. Then Ragar snorted. 'She'll grow out of it.'

So there was a crack after all. A daughter. A girl barely older than a child who still had a conscience her father had lost.

'Kian's still buying,' Ragar said, steering the conversation back to business. 'All the birds we can bring him. Says there's more coin in it now. Demand's up. Some magika wants them by the dozen.'

Caelen's pulse hammered against his throat. *Birds.* They called them birds, as if Jonah had been nothing more than a crow to be swatted from the sky.

'We go tonight,' Garik said, and Caelen heard the resignation in it. The exhaustion of a man caught in a trap of his own making. 'One more run. Then I'm done for a while. Need to... I don't know. Need to think.'

The words rang in Caelen's ears. *Tonight. Again.*

His pulse hammered so hard he could feel it in his fingertips, in his jaw, behind his eyes. He thought of Jonah. Of blood on leaves. Of beaks cut clean and heads taken as trophies.

He imagined drawing his dagger, right here, right now. How fast it would be. How the blade would feel sliding between Ragar's ribs. How short his own life would become in the chaos that followed.

Too many eyes. Too many bodies. Too many witnesses.

He forced himself to breathe through his nose, slow and controlled.

His hand shook once—hard enough that the mug tilted, ale sloshing over the rim and onto his knuckles. The liquid was cold, shocking against his skin. He set the cup down too fast; the base cracked against the table with a sharp clink that drew a few glances from nearby tables.

He muttered an apology under his breath, rose without looking back at the hunters, and pushed through the door into the street.

Cold air hit him like a physical blow. He bent forward, hands on his knees, breathing hard until the red haze cleared from his vision and the pounding in his ears eased to something manageable.

Inside, the tavern roared on. The hunters drinking. Planning. Laughing, probably.

They were hunting again.

Tonight.

While the village sat behind its wards and waited for salvation that would never come.

Caelen straightened slowly. His hands still shook, but his feet were steady when he moved back into the square. The noise, the carts, the shouting—none of it blurred together anymore. Every detail stood sharp and clear.

He had come to Wyntown for answers.

He had found them.

Now he had to decide what they would cost.

And whether he was willing to pay.

# CHAPTER FOUR

*The Bridge*

As Caelen neared Bearwater Bridge on his way back from Wyntown, his gaze landed on a figure by the river's edge—a young girl, her body shaking with silent sobs.

He froze, instinct screaming at him to keep walking. Getting involved with humans was dangerous enough without drawing attention to himself. But something about the way she huddled there, so utterly alone, made him pause.

He swept his eyes over the surroundings, searching for threats. The road was empty. The bridge stood quiet. Only the gentle murmur of the river and the occasional croak of frogs broke the silence.

Slowly, carefully, he approached.

'Hey,' he called out softly, not wanting to startle her. 'Are you alright?'

She didn't turn. Didn't acknowledge him. Just kept staring at the water as if it held answers she desperately needed.

As he drew closer, his stomach turned. A bruise marked her shoulder—dark and unmistakable, the clear shape of a handprint stark against the pale blue fabric of her dress. More marks crisscrossed her exposed arms. Fresh ones, angry and red.

'What happened to you?' The words came out before he could stop them, concern overriding caution.

'None of your business!' Her voice cracked with the effort of sounding strong. She turned her tear-streaked face toward the water, refusing to look at him. The trembling in her shoulders betrayed her attempt at defiance.

Caelen felt a pang of recognition. He knew that kind of hurt. The kind that made you want to disappear. The kind that came from people who were supposed to protect you.

He sank down into the grass several feet away, giving her space but making it clear he wasn't leaving. 'Alright. I won't pry.'

The silence stretched between them, filled only by the river's voice and the frogs singing their twilight chorus. He studied her from the corner of his eye—the dirt and sweat marring what had once been a clean dress, the way she held herself too carefully, as if any movement might shatter something already broken.

'Would you mind if I just... sat here?' he ventured. 'You don't have to talk. I just—' He struggled to find words that wouldn't sound foolish. 'It's hard for me to see someone hurting and just walk away.'

For a long moment, she said nothing.

Then, gradually, she lifted her face. Blonde hair clung damp to her tear-stained cheeks. She swiped at her eyes with the back of her hand, tucking the tangled strands behind her ear with trembling fingers.

When her eyes met his, Caelen's breath caught.

Blue. The clearest, most striking blue he'd ever seen—like the sky on a winter morning, bright and sharp and impossibly sad.

'Who are you?' she asked, her voice barely above a whisper.

'Caelen.' The name came easily. The rest—where he was from, what he was—stayed locked behind his teeth. 'I'm... traveling through. From the west.'

'I've never seen you before.' She studied him with the wariness of someone who'd learned not to trust easily.

'Just arrived.' He kept his voice gentle, his posture open and un-threatening. 'My name's Caelen,' he said again, as if repetition might make him seem less foreign, less dangerous.

'Leira.'

The name hit him like a physical blow.

*Leira.*

The poacher's daughter. Garik's child. The girl he'd heard about in the tavern, the one who couldn't look at her father anymore because of what he did.

A flood of emotions threatened to drown him—anger at her father, shock at finding her here, sympathy for the pain clearly written on her skin. He wrestled with the contradictions, trying to reconcile this vulnerable, hurting girl with the brutal hunter he'd been plan-ning to... what? Confront? Kill?

She shivered, and he realized she was soaked through. The evening was growing cold, mist rising from the river.

'You're freezing.' He unfastened his cloak without waiting for per-mission and moved closer, draping it over her shoulders. The fabric swallowed her small frame, making her look even younger than six-teen.

She pulled it tight around herself, and for the first time, something like gratitude flickered across her face. 'Thank you.'

'How long have you been out here?'

'Since yesterday evening.' Her voice was hollow. 'Couldn't go home. Couldn't stay. So I just... walked. Ended up here.'

A full day and night. No food. No shelter. Just sitting by the river, too afraid or too stubborn to go back.

'What happened?' Caelen asked quietly. 'You don't have to tell me if you don't want to. But sometimes it helps. Talking to someone who doesn't know all the history.'

She stared across the river at the forest—the same forest Caelen called home, though she didn't know that. When she spoke, her voice was distant, as if she were telling someone else's story.

'My father believes he's justified. That what he does is necessary. Survival, he calls it.' She laughed, a broken sound. 'But he refuses to see—refuses to even acknowledge—that it's wrong.'

Caelen sat very still, barely breathing, letting her speak.

'He works with his brother. Ragar. They go into the forest and—' Her voice caught. She didn't finish the sentence.

She didn't need to. Caelen already knew.

He placed a careful hand on her shoulder, feeling her whole body tense at the contact before slowly, incrementally, relaxing. She bowed her head and wept—not the silent tears from before, but deep, wrenching sobs that shook her entire frame.

He didn't say anything. Didn't offer empty platitudes. Just sat there, his hand steady on her shoulder, while she cried out some of the poison that had been building inside her.

When the sobs finally subsided, she wiped her eyes with the edge of his cloak and looked at him with something almost like wonder.

'You're not from around here,' she said. 'Are you?'

'No.'

'Good. Then you don't know how things are. Don't know about ...' She gestured vaguely toward the town. 'All of this.'

'Tell me,' he said. 'If you want to.'

She took a shaky breath. 'They hunt the Arvi. The skin-changers. The raven people.' The words came out quiet but steady now, as if saying them out loud was both terrifying and necessary. 'For dark magikas who pay in gold. It's cruel. It's murder. And my father—' Her voice broke again. 'My father comes home with blood on his hands and expects me to smile and thank him for keeping us fed.'

Caelen's throat tightened. She knew. She understood what her father did, and it was tearing her apart.

'I tried to tell him it was wrong,' she continued. 'Last night. I told him I'd rather starve than live on blood money. That the Arvi are people, not animals to be harvested.' She touched the bruise on her shoulder without seeming to realize it. 'He didn't take it well.'

White-hot rage flooded through Caelen. Garik had hurt her. His own daughter. Because she'd dared to have a conscience.

'He hurt you.' It wasn't a question.

'He's never—' She stopped, reconsidered. 'He's never been like this before. The hunting, it's... it's changing him. Making him into someone I don't recognize. Someone who can look at a child and see coin instead of a person. Someone who can—' She broke off, fresh tears spilling down her cheeks.

Caelen found himself caught in her gaze, those impossibly blue eyes holding him like a spell. His anger at her father ebbed, not disappearing but transforming into something else. Something protective. Determined.

Not all humans were monsters. This girl proved it.

'Leira!' A voice boomed from the direction of town.

They both spun, scrambling to their feet as two figures approached across the bridge.

Garik and Ragar. Moving fast, their faces twisted with anger.

Caelen's hand moved instinctively toward the knife hidden beneath his shirt, but he forced himself to stay still. *Too many witnesses. Too much daylight. Control yourself.*

'Leira, what are you doing out here?' Garik's voice was rough, but Caelen heard something underneath the anger. Worry. Fear. 'And who's this?'

He advanced, Ragar half a step behind, both of them radiating threat. Garik's face was flushed red, the veins in his neck bulging with barely controlled fury.

But his eyes—when they landed on his daughter—held a flicker of something else. Guilt, maybe. Or shame.

'Leira, get back to the house now,' Garik barked. 'You have chores.'

'I said now!' Garik's voice cracked like a whip.

Leira turned to Caelen, her eyes apologetic. She unwrapped his cloak and held it out. 'Thank you,' she said softly. Her voice carried layers of meaning—for the warmth, for listening, for not judging her.

Their fingers brushed as he took the cloak back, and Caelen felt his pulse jump.

'Stay away from my daughter.' Garik was suddenly in front of him, invading his space. He poked Caelen's shoulder hard with one finger, the jab sharp enough to sting. 'You hear me, boy?'

Up close, Garik smelled of old sweat and stale ale. His breath was sour. But his eyes—those were what caught Caelen's attention. Bloodshot. Haunted. The eyes of a man who wasn't sleeping well.

Good.

Caelen bit down on the inside of his cheek, using the pain to keep himself silent.

He wouldn't give them one.

'I mean it,' Garik said, leaning in close. 'Stay away from her. She doesn't need some drifter putting ideas in her head.'

Caelen met his eyes and held them, saying nothing. Let the hunter see what he wanted to see—a harmless traveler, cowed and backing down.

After a long, tense moment, Garik stepped back. He grabbed Leira's arm—not gently, but not roughly either—and turned away.

Caelen watched them go. Leira looked back once, her blue eyes finding his across the growing distance. She mouthed something that might have been 'sorry' or 'help' or just 'goodbye.'

Then they were gone, disappearing into the streets of Wyntown.

Caelen stood alone on the bridge, his hands shaking with suppressed rage. A newfound hatred for Garik burned in his chest, made worse by the complication Leira represented.

She was the daughter of the man who'd killed Jonah. The child of a murderer.

But she was also a victim. A girl who saw the truth of what her father did and hated him for it. A girl with a conscience in a place that seemed to have forgotten what conscience meant.

And those eyes...

He shook his head, trying to clear the image from his mind. This was dangerous territory. Getting involved with her meant getting close to Garik, meant risking discovery, meant complicating everything.

But he couldn't shake the memory of her huddled by the river, alone and hurting.

Or the bruises on her skin.

Or the way she'd looked at him like he was the first person in a long time who'd treated her like she mattered.

Caelen turned and crossed the bridge, heading back toward the forest. Back toward home and safety.

But his thoughts stayed behind, tangled up in blonde hair and blue eyes and the impossible situation he'd just walked into.

The instant Caelen crossed the threshold into his family's dwelling, he knew he was in trouble.

His parents stood in the center of the room, their forms rigid with worry and barely contained anger. His mother's hands were white-knuckled where they gripped her apron. His father's jaw was set in a way Caelen knew meant the shouting would start soon.

The smell of his mother's fresh-baked bread filled the space—normally a comfort, now just a reminder of the home he'd abandoned to chase information in Wyntown.

Candlelight threw harsh shadows across his father's face as he turned. 'Caelen!' The word cracked like thunder. 'Where in the name of the forest have you been?'

'I need you to listen—' Caelen started, but his father cut him off.

'Listen? *Listen?* Do you have any idea how worried we've been? Your mother has been sick with fear!'

'I went to Wyntown,' Caelen said, forcing the words out before courage could fail him. 'I had to know. About the hunters. About what they're planning.'

The silence that followed was worse than the shouting.

His mother's hand flew to her mouth, her eyes going wide with horror. 'Wyntown? You went into a *human settlement?*' Her voice climbed with each word. 'Caelen, what were you thinking?'

'I was thinking that hiding and waiting isn't working!' The frustration he'd been holding since the village meeting burst out. 'Three of us have disappeared in the last month. Jonah is dead. And the elders want us to just... wait. Hope they stop. Hope they forget about us. Well, they're not stopping. And I needed to know why.'

'You could have been killed!' His father's voice was ice-cold now, which was somehow worse than the anger. 'You walked into their territory, alone, without weapons, without backup. One wrong move, one shadow falling wrong, and you'd be the next name we're mourning.'

'But I wasn't—'

'By sheer luck!' His father slammed his hand on the table, making the dishes jump. 'You survived by luck, not skill. And what did this reckless gamble gain us? What information was worth risking your life for?'

Caelen drew a breath, steadying himself. 'I know when they're hunting next. Tonight. And I know why the attacks have increased.'

That got their attention. His mother sank into a chair, her face pale. His father's expression shifted from anger to something more complex.

'Tell us,' his father said quietly. 'Everything.'

So Caelen did. He told them about the cart ride, about the tavern, about overhearing Garik and Ragar. His mother gasped when he mentioned the hunters by name. His father's hands clenched and unclenched as Caelen described the plan to hunt again tonight.

'And there's more,' Caelen said. 'They mentioned a magika. Volthar. He's paying them—paying all the hunters—to bring him as many of us as they can. That's why the attacks have gotten worse. It's not random hunting anymore. It's systematic harvest.'

His father's face went gray. 'Volthar,' he repeated, the name hanging in the air like a curse.

'You know the name?'

'Old stories. Very old.' His father exchanged a look with his mother that Caelen couldn't read. 'If that magika has turned his attention to our people... we need to tell the elders immediately.'

'I tried!' Caelen's frustration bubbled up again. 'At the meeting, remember? But Illdran doesn't want to hear about fighting back. Doesn't want to hear about doing anything except hiding and hoping.'

'Because fighting has never worked for us!' His father's voice rose again. 'Our people tried that once. It ended in slaughter. That's why there are so few of us left. That's why we hide. Not because we're cowards, but because we're the last survivors of a war we lost.'

'Then we're already dead,' Caelen said quietly. 'We're just waiting for them to finish the job.'

His mother made a small, pained sound.

His father's expression crumbled, fury giving way to something like despair. 'You're so young,' he said. 'You think rage and righteous anger are enough. That wanting to fight makes you brave. But I've lived longer, seen more. I know that sometimes survival means swallowing your pride. Biding your time. Waiting for the right moment instead of charging in like a fool.'

'And if the right moment never comes?'

'Then at least you're alive to keep waiting.' His father turned away, his shoulders slumped. 'I won't lose you to some pointless heroic gesture, Caelen. I won't bury my son because he thought he could take on an army of hunters with nothing but anger and good intentions.'

The words stung more than any blow could have.

'Your father's right,' his mother said softly. She'd stopped crying, but her eyes were still red. 'We can't fight them, Caelen. We don't have the numbers. We don't have the weapons. All we have is the forest and the wards and each other. That has to be enough.'

'But it's not,' Caelen whispered. 'It's not enough. Jonah is dead. And tonight they're going hunting again, and someone else is going to die, and we're going to sit here and do nothing.'

His father turned back, and there was something fierce in his eyes now. 'We'll tell Illdran. Let the elders decide what to do with your information. But you—' He pointed at Caelen. 'You are not leaving this village tonight. You're not going near Wyntown, not going near the hunters, not putting yourself in danger. Do you understand?'

It wasn't really a question.

'Yes, sir,' Caelen said, the words tasting like ash.

His mother stood and pulled him into a tight embrace. 'We can't lose you,' she whispered against his hair. 'You're all we have. Please, Caelen. Please be careful.'

He hugged her back, feeling the trembling in her shoulders, and some of his anger drained away. They weren't trying to stop him out of cowardice. They were scared. Terrified of losing their only child the way so many families had lost theirs.

'Come on,' his father said, his voice softer now. 'Let's go see Illdran. Tell him what you learned. Maybe...' He trailed off, not finishing the thought.

Maybe it would make a difference. Maybe the elders would act. Maybe knowing about Volthar would change things.

Caelen didn't believe it. But he followed his parents out the door anyway.

They walked through the village as twilight deepened into night. Neighbors watched them pass with curious eyes. Word would spread quickly—the boy who'd gone to Wyntown, the family walking to the elder's home with grim faces.

His mother knocked heavily on Illdran's door.

'One moment,' came the muffled reply.

They waited in silence, Caelen's father with one hand on his shoulder—whether for comfort or to keep him from bolting, Caelen wasn't sure.

The door opened to reveal Illdran's smiling face. 'Oh, hello Loreleia and Cae—' The smile faltered as he took in their expressions. 'Come in. Please.'

They filed into the small dwelling. The aroma of hot soup filled the air, making Caelen's empty stomach growl. He realized he hadn't eaten since yesterday.

'We need to talk,' Loreleia said without preamble. 'Caelen, tell him what you told us.'

So for the third time that day, Caelen recounted his journey to Wyntown. Illdran listened with occasional gasps and tuts of disapproval, his expression growing more troubled with each detail.

When Caelen finished, the elder was quiet for a long moment, adjusting the spectacles perched on the end of his nose.

'That is quite the tale, young one,' Illdran said finally. 'Venturing into a human settlement was extraordinarily rash. You could have been discovered. Killed. Or worse—captured and used to lead them back to us.'

'But I wasn't,' Caelen said. 'And now we know—'

'Know what? That hunters are hunting? That they're being paid well for it?' Illdran's voice was gentle but firm. 'We already knew these things, Caelen. The specifics don't change our situation.'

'But Volthar—'

'Is a name I hoped never to hear again.'

The words hung in the air like a death knell.

Caelen leaned forward. 'You know him? You know who he is?'

Illdran's expression shifted, something dark passing behind his eyes. For a moment, the kindly elder disappeared, replaced by someone who'd seen terrible things.

'I know of him,' Illdran said carefully. 'The name is old. Very old. There are stories, legends really, about a magika who sought power through forbidden means. Who experimented on living things to fuel his magic. Who was driven out of every settlement he tried to make home because even other humans feared what he'd become.' He removed his spectacles and cleaned them with shaking hands. 'But those are old tales. Bedtime stories to frighten children. Surely it can't be the same—'

'He's real,' Caelen insisted. 'The hunters spoke of him like he was real. Like he's out there right now, paying them gold for our bodies.'

'Then we're in more danger than I feared.' Illdran replaced his spectacles and stood, pacing the small room. 'If Volthar has truly returned, if he's hunting our people specifically... we need to convene the full council. Tonight.'

'What will you tell them?' Caelen's father asked.

'The truth. What Caelen learned. And what I know from the old stories.' Illdran turned to Caelen with an expression that was almost apologetic. 'You did a brave thing today, going to Wyntown. A foolish thing, but brave. The information you gathered is valuable. But it also confirms our worst fears—that we're not facing random hunters anymore, but an organized effort backed by powerful magic.'

'So what do we do?' Caelen asked.

'We survive. We endure. We wait for—'

'For what?' Caelen couldn't keep the frustration from his voice. 'For Volthar to collect enough of us? For the hunters to find the village? How long do we wait before waiting becomes suicide?'

Illdran's face hardened. 'Trouble yourself no more with this matter, Caelen. Go home. Stay with your mother. Let the elders handle this.'

It was a dismissal, gentle but absolute.

'Thank you for seeing us, Illdran,' Loreleia said, placing a hand on Caelen's arm and guiding him toward the door.

'The council will meet at midnight,' Illdran said. 'We'll send word of our decision in the morning.'

The door closed behind them with a soft click that sounded like finality.

Outside, Caelen's mother turned to him. 'No more journeys to the humans, Caelen. I mean it.' Her expression was iron. 'Promise me. No more risks.'

Caelen looked at his parents—at his mother's fear-bright eyes, at his father's weary resignation. They wanted him to promise safety. To choose survival over action.

'I promise,' he said.

It was a lie.

His thoughts were already back across the bridge, tangled up in a girl with blonde hair and blue eyes. A girl who was trapped in a house with a man who'd hurt her for having a conscience. A girl whose father would go hunting again tonight, would kill more of Caelen's people, while the elders met and talked and decided to do nothing.

Leira.

The name echoed in his mind like a prayer or a curse, he wasn't sure which.

He'd promised to stay away from humans. To stay safe.

But some promises were meant to be broken.

# CHAPTER FIVE

*Blood and Silence*

Night cloaked Wyntown in shadow as Garik approached his brother's house. The small cottage sat on a rise overlooking the river, its windows dark save for a single candle burning in the front room.

He'd promised himself he wouldn't do this. Had spent the day after Leira fled trying to convince himself there was another way. That he could change, could find different work, could become the father she needed him to be.

But the debts didn't disappear because he'd developed a conscience. The roof still leaked. His sister's children still needed food. And Ragar was waiting.

'Ready to go?' Garik asked, his voice rough as gravel.

Ragar emerged from the doorway, already loaded with gear—nets, traps, the Earthbind flares that cost a small fortune but made the work possible. He grinned, the expression sharp in the candlelight.

'Aye, just making sure the traps are secure.' He hefted the pack with practiced ease. 'So where are we heading this time?'

Garik felt ice settle in his gut as he spoke the words he'd been rehearsing all day. 'Deeper. Into their territory. We need to find the villages, get close enough to—' He stopped, the sentence dying in his throat.

*Get close enough to what? To slaughter them in their homes? To make Leira hate you even more than she already does?*

'To what?' Ragar prompted.

'To corner a few lone ones,' Garik finished. 'Quietly. No commotion. In and out before they know we're there.'

It was what they'd done before, in the early days when the hunting was easier and his conscience quieter. Find a solitary raven away from the protection of their kin, use the Earthbind, make the capture quick and clean.

Except it was never clean. Not really.

'Solid plan,' Ragar said, slinging the pack over his shoulder. 'Sounds easy enough.'

Garik scoffed, though whether at his brother's confidence or his own participation, he wasn't sure. 'Let's move. We're heading north, right? To that village... what's it called, chorlora?'

'Caelora,' Ragar corrected with a laugh. 'How many times do I have to tell you?'

'Right. Caelora.' The name tasted like ash in his mouth. A village. A community. Families and children and people who were probably sitting down to evening meals right now, unaware that two hunters were planning to raid them.

*People*, his mind insisted. *Not birds. Not animals. People.*

He pushed the thought away and shouldered his share of the gear. The metal traps were cold even through the fabric of his pack, their hollow clinks echoing through the quiet street as they walked.

The night was darker than usual, heavy clouds swallowing the moon and stars. Their torches carved trembling circles of light through the blackness as they crossed the old wooden bridge. The scent of burning pine mixed with the river's dampness, following them as they entered the forest.

Garik had walked this path a hundred times. Knew every root and stone, every place where the ground turned treacherous. But tonight, it felt different. Wrong, somehow. As if the forest itself knew what they planned and disapproved.

*You're being foolish*, he told himself. *It's just trees. Just darkness. Nothing more.*

But he couldn't shake the feeling of being watched.

Two hours of hard walking brought them to the outskirts of Caelora.

Garik raised a hand, signaling Ragar to stop. They doused their torches and crept closer, keeping to the shadows, hearts hammering against ribs.

What they saw made Garik's breath catch.

The village wasn't primitive or savage as the stories claimed. Structures of woven branches and living wood rose organically from the forest floor, lit by soft lanterns that cast golden light across well-maintained paths. Ravens—both the human-shaped and bird-formed—moved through the streets with casual ease. Children laughed somewhere in the distance. The smell of cooking food drifted on the evening air.

It looked like home.

*Because it is home*, something whispered in his mind. *Their home. Which you're about to violate.*

'Would you look at that,' Ragar breathed, his voice thick with something Garik recognized as greed. 'There must be dozens of them here. Maybe more.'

'Keep your voice down,' Garik hissed.

But Ragar wasn't listening, his eyes tracking the movements of the villagers with the focus of a predator sizing up prey. 'You thinking what I'm thinking, brother?'

'That we need to be careful and get out alive?'

'That we're looking at a fortune.' Ragar's grin was predatory in the darkness. 'With a few more men, we could take this whole village in one night. Can you imagine? The gold Volthar would pay for a haul like that?'

The suggestion hit Garik like a physical blow. A raid. Not hunting stragglers, but attacking the village itself. Women. Children. Families.

He thought of Leira's words: *Someone who can look at a child and see coin instead of a person.*

'We're not doing that,' Garik said flatly.

'Why not? They're right there, Garik. Undefended. Ripe for the taking.'

'I said no.' The words came out harder than he intended. 'We stick to the plan. One target. Quick and quiet.'

Ragar studied him in the darkness, suspicion flickering across his face. 'You're getting soft.'

'I'm being smart. You want to attack a whole village? How many of them you think would fight back? How many hunters you think would die trying?' Garik shook his head. 'We take one. Make our coin. Live to hunt another day.'

It was practical reasoning. Logical. It had nothing to do with the way his stomach turned at the thought of slaughtering these people in their homes.

Nothing at all.

After a long moment, Ragar grunted agreement. 'Fine. But we're discussing this later. That kind of opportunity doesn't come around often.'

They hunkered down behind a thick screen of foliage, watching. Waiting.

A woman emerged from one of the dwellings—middle-aged, dark-haired, carrying a lantern. She moved toward a small outbuilding at the edge of the village, alone and unguarded.

'There,' Ragar whispered, already reaching for his net. 'Perfect.'

Garik watched her walk, noted the tired set of her shoulders, the way she paused to adjust her shawl against the evening chill. Someone's wife. Someone's mother. Someone who probably had people waiting for her to come back.

Just like Leira waited for him.

Used to wait for him.

'Garik?' Ragar's voice pulled him back. 'You with me?'

No. He wasn't. He wanted to be anywhere but here, doing anything but this.

But he nodded anyway.

They moved through the trees like smoke, years of practice making them nearly silent. Garik positioned himself on one side of the small building while Ragar crouched by the door, net ready.

The plan was simple. Wait for her to emerge. Throw the net. Pour the Wing-Bane down her throat and make her transform. Disappear into the forest before anyone noticed.

Simple. Clean. Quick.

Garik's hands were shaking.

He heard movement inside the structure. Saw Ragar tense, preparing. Gave the signal—a quick nod.

The door opened.

The woman stepped out, still holding her lantern, humming softly under her breath. The tune was gentle, familiar somehow. A lullaby, maybe.

Ragar moved with brutal efficiency. The net flew through the air, tangling around her before she could react. She drew breath to scream—

Garik was there, one hand clamping over her mouth while the other fumbled for the vial at his belt. Her eyes went wide with terror, meeting his in the lamplight. Dark eyes. Terrified. *Human* eyes.

He poured the Wing-Bane down her throat, felt her body convulse as the transformation was forced upon her. Watched as she shrank, shifted, became a black-feathered bird thrashing in the net.

It was quick. It was clean.

It made him want to vomit.

'Move!' Ragar hissed, already gathering the netted bird and running for the treeline.

Behind them, a man emerged from the house—tall, broad-shouldered, calling a name. Tyrae. The woman's name was Tyrae.

The man shifted mid-stride, becoming a raven in a burst of feathers, taking to the air in pursuit.

'Faster!' Garik gasped, crashing through the undergrowth.

The forest became a maze of shadows and obstacles. Branches lashed at his face. Roots tried to trip him. Behind them, he could hear the pursuing raven's harsh cries, could feel the rush of wings.

They ran until Garik's lungs burned, until his legs screamed for mercy, until the sounds of pursuit finally faded.

When they stopped, doubled over and gasping, Ragar was grinning.

The netted raven—Tyrae—was still struggling, making distressed sounds that were too intelligent, too frightened to be simply animal.

'Do it quick,' Garik managed, not looking at the bird. At her. At what they'd reduced her to.

Ragar pulled out his knife.

Garik turned away before the blade fell. But he heard it. Heard the wet sound of steel through feather and bone. Heard the moment the struggling stopped.

Silence.

Then Ragar's triumphant laugh. 'That was close! But we did it, brother. Clean capture.'

'Yeah.' Garik's voice sounded hollow to his own ears. 'Clean.'

'You know what I was thinking?' Ragar was already moving forward, planning ahead like the woman they'd just killed was already forgotten. 'If we had a few more men—just a handful—we could take that whole village in one go. With the right strategy, enough swords...'

He kept talking, spinning out his vision of organized slaughter, but Garik barely heard him.

All he could think about was the woman's eyes. The way she'd looked at him in that final moment before the Wing-Bane took hold. The terror. The betrayal.

The same look Leira had given him before she fled into the night.

'I'll take care of it,' Garik heard himself say. 'Recruiting more hunters. I'll handle it.'

Ragar clapped him on the shoulder. 'That's the spirit! Knew I could count on you.'

But as they made their way back through the forest, Tyrae's body wrapped in canvas and slung over Ragar's shoulder like a hunting trophy, Garik felt something crack inside him.

He'd crossed a line tonight. Knew it with absolute certainty.

The question was whether he'd ever be able to cross back.

CAELEN

The room was dark save for a single candle guttering on the table beside his bed. Caelen lay sprawled across rough wool blankets, staring at the ceiling's wooden beams without really seeing them.

He couldn't sleep. Couldn't stop thinking about Leira's blue eyes, about the bruise on her shoulder, about the way she'd looked at him like he was the first person in months to treat her like a human being.

About how her father was out there right now, hunting Caelen's people.

The elders had met at midnight as promised: *We will increase patrols. Wait and watch.*

Wait and watch while the hunters picked them off one by one.

Caelen's hands clenched into fists.

Outside, the village was settling into uneasy sleep. The normal sounds of evening—conversation, laughter, the rustling of wings as people shifted form before roosting—had a nervous edge tonight. Everyone knew the hunters were getting bolder. Everyone felt the noose tightening.

But knowing and acting were different things.

A sound split the night—a scream, raw and terrible.

'They took her! They took her!'

Caelen was off his bed and out the door before conscious thought caught up, his heart hammering against his ribs.

The village square was filling rapidly, people emerging from their homes in various states of dress and transformation. At the center of the growing crowd knelt Galaeron—a man Caelen knew by sight if not name, married to Tyrae, one of the village's weavers.

He was sobbing, his face buried in his hands, his entire body shaking.

'They took her,' he kept repeating, the words broken and raw. 'They took her.'

Illdran pushed through the crowd, moving with the speed of someone younger than his years. He knelt beside Galaeron, placing a weathered hand on the man's shoulder.

'Galaeron. Breathe. Tell me what happened.'

The man raised his head slowly. His eyes were red-rimmed, drowning in tears. Long hair hung loose around his face, normally neat but now wild with distress.

'Poachers,' he choked out. 'She went to the outhouse. I was inside, waiting for her to come back. When she didn't, I went to check and—' His voice broke. 'They had her. In a net. I shifted, tried to chase them, but they were too fast. Too prepared. I lost them in the trees and when I came back...'

He held up his hands. They were covered in blood. Not his own.

'I found where they'd stopped. Found her. What was left of her.'

A collective gasp rippled through the crowd. Someone cried out. Others pressed hands to mouths, eyes wide with horror.

Caelen felt ice flood his veins. Tyrae. He remembered her—quiet woman, skilled at her craft, always had a kind word for the children. Gone. Murdered.

While the elders waited and watched.

'Are you certain they were poachers?' Illdran's voice was gentle but insistent, as if hoping the answer might change.

Galaeron's laugh was bitter, broken. 'What else would they be? They had nets. Earthbind. They knew exactly what they were doing. This wasn't random. This was a *raid*.'

The word sent a shudder through the crowd. Raids meant organization. Planning. It meant the hunters were escalating.

Two village women stepped forward, gently helping Galaeron to his feet, supporting him between them. His legs barely held him. He looked like a man whose world had just ended.

Because it had.

Illdran turned to face the crowd, raising his hands for calm. 'Please, everyone. I know you're frightened. I know this is terrible. But we must not panic. We must think clearly—'

'Think clearly?' The voice came from somewhere in the back. 'We've been thinking clearly for months while they pick us off! How much clearer does it need to get?'

Murmurs of agreement rippled through the assembly.

'We don't know with absolute certainty that—' Illdran began.

'You heard what he said!' Another voice, angrier. 'They raided us. Came right to the village edge. Tyrae is dead. What more proof do you need?'

The crowd was getting restless now, fear transmuting into anger. Caelen could feel it building, could see it in the clenched fists and hard eyes of his neighbors.

'We must act,' someone shouted. Others took up the cry, voices overlapping, demands growing louder.

Caelen stood at the edge of the crowd, watching Illdran try to calm the rising tide of fury. Watching him fail.

The same old words. The same empty promises. Wait. Watch. Be patient.

While Tyrae's blood was still wet on Galaeron's hands.

Something broke inside Caelen.

He pushed forward through the crowd, his voice cutting through the chaos. 'What are you scared of?'

The square fell silent. Every head turned toward him.

Illdran blinked, clearly startled. 'Caelen—'

'No.' Caelen cut him off. His heart was pounding, but the words came anyway, unstoppable. 'What else needs to happen before you act? How many more have to die? Mara? Corvus? Elara? Jonah? Now Tyrae? How long is this list going to get before you finally do something?'

'You don't understand what you're asking,' Illdran said, his voice tight with controlled anger. 'You're young. You don't remember—'

'I remember Jonah,' Caelen snapped. 'I remember hearing of them carrying his head away like a trophy. I remember his mother's face when she learned he was dead. I remember every single person we've lost because we're too afraid to fight back!'

The crowd stirred. Some nodded. Others looked uncertain.

'We can't afford to wait any longer,' Caelen continued, his voice rising. 'They're not going to stop. They're getting bolder, coming closer. Tonight they raided the village edge. Tomorrow they might come for the center. How many more of us have to die before you admit that hiding isn't working?'

Illdran's face hardened. 'Do you yearn for bloodshed, boy? Are you so eager to start a war? To watch your friends die? Your family? Because that's what you're asking for.'

'We're already at war!' The words exploded out of Caelen. 'You just haven't accepted it yet!'

Silence crashed over the square.

Everyone stared—at Caelen, at Illdran, at the impossible tension stretched between them.

Illdran's expression went cold. 'Insolent child,' he said quietly. Then louder, to the crowd: 'Go home. All of you. There will be an emergency council meeting at dawn. We will discuss our options. But I will not have panic drive us to rash decisions.'

He turned and walked away, his back rigid with anger.

The crowd began to disperse, breaking into small groups that continued arguing in hushed, urgent tones. Some shot Caelen approving looks. Others avoided his eyes, clearly uncomfortable with his challenge to the elder's authority.

His father was suddenly there, gripping his arm. 'Caelen. You can't speak to Illdran like that. He's an elder. You need to show respect.'

'Respect?' Caelen yanked his arm free, the fury still burning hot in his chest. 'What respect is he showing us by doing nothing? What respect did Tyrae get tonight?'

'That's not fair—'

'It's completely fair!' Caelen's voice cracked. 'She's dead. She's dead because we hide and hope and pray the hunters will just... what? Get bored? Find a new target? It's not working, Father. Can't you see that?'

His mother stepped forward, tears on her cheeks. 'Caelen, please—'

'No.' He stepped back, shaking his head. 'I'm done. I'm done waiting for permission to survive.'

He turned and walked away, his parents' calls following him into the darkness.

His father's voice rang out one last time: 'Leave him be.' Then softer, to his mother: 'He needs to cool down.'

But Caelen wasn't going to cool down. The rage burning in his chest felt like the only warm thing in a world gone cold with fear and indecision.

Tyrae was dead.

The hunters would strike again.

And the elders would do nothing.

Unless someone forced their hand.

Caelen disappeared into the shadows at the village's edge, his mind already racing ahead to dangerous possibilities. To choices that couldn't be undone.

To a girl with blonde hair and blue eyes whose father had just murdered one of his people.

The night stretched ahead, full of terrible potential.

And for the first time since Jonah died, Caelen felt like he might actually be able to do something about it.

# CHAPTER SIX

## *The Trap*

The lantern outside the tavern cast wavering light across wet cobblestones, its glow catching in puddles like scattered coins. Garik found Jeremiah where he always was this time of night—on the weathered bench outside, whittling a piece of wood with hands that had once been steady as stone.

From inside the tavern came waves of raucous laughter, the clinking of mugs, the smell of roasted meat and spilled ale. Normal sounds. The sounds of men who weren't planning mass murder.

Garik's stomach turned.

He'd barely slept since last night. Kept seeing Tyrae's eyes in the moment before the Wing-Bane took hold. Kept hearing the wet sound of Ragar's knife. Kept thinking about Leira's words: *Someone who can look at a child and see coin instead of a person.*

But he was here anyway. Because debts didn't pay themselves. Because Ragar was right—a raid on the village meant enough gold to be free of this life forever. One last job, then he could change. Could become the father Leira needed.

That's what he told himself.

'Garik.' Jeremiah didn't look up from his whittling, the blade scraping rhythmically against wood. 'How'd the hunt go?'

'Could've been better.' The words tasted like ash. 'I need to talk to you about something.'

Now Jeremiah did look up, his weathered face sharp despite the years. He'd been one of the best hunters in the region before a raven had torn up his leg during a botched capture five years back. Now he recruited and planned while younger men did the actual work.

'What's on your mind, lad?'

Garik knelt down, meeting the old hunter's eyes. His heart hammered against his ribs. This was it—the moment he crossed from hunter to something worse. 'We need a different approach. The ravens are getting too careful. Too hard to catch one at a time.'

'That so?' Jeremiah set down his knife, giving Garik his full attention. 'What are you proposing?'

The night air was cool, carrying the distant call of an owl and the rich scent of damp earth. Garik felt every sound, every smell with unnatural clarity, as if the world were trying to make him notice this moment. Mark it as important.

'A raid,' he said quietly. 'On their village. We hit them at night, use Earthbind to trap them in human form, cage them, and get out before they can organize a defense.'

Jeremiah's eyebrows rose. 'Bold. Very bold.' He leaned back, studying Garik's face. 'Also extremely dangerous. Those birds aren't stupid. They'll fight.'

'I know. That's why we need more men. Overwhelming force, in and out quick.' Garik's voice was steady, but his hands wanted to shake. 'Are you in?'

A long pause. Jeremiah stroked his beard, his eyes distant. 'How many men?'

'Seven more. Plus you for planning, me and Ragar for leading. Ten total.'

'You'll need a lot of potion for that. Earthbind isn't cheap, and if you're planning to force-shift them...' Jeremiah whistled low. 'That's a small fortune in Wing-Bane.'

'I'll handle the potions. You handle recruitment.' Garik stood, needing to move, needing to not think about what he was planning. 'Get men who can keep their mouths shut and their nerve steady. We move tomorrow night.'

'Tomorrow?' Jeremiah's eyes sharpened. 'That's fast.'

'Before word spreads. Before they can prepare.' Before I lose my nerve. 'Can you do it?'

Jeremiah was quiet for a long moment, then nodded slowly. 'I can get seven men who'll follow orders and not ask too many questions. But Garik—' He caught Garik's arm as he turned to leave. 'You sure about this? Raiding a village... that's different from hunting strays. That's war.'

*We're already at war.*

The boy—Caelen—had said that. Young raven who'd challenged his elder in the village square, calling for action while the old ones counselled patience.

Maybe he'd been right.

'I'm sure,' Garik said, pulling free of Jeremiah's grip. 'Tomorrow night. Have them ready.'

He walked away before the old hunter could ask any more questions. Before Garik had to explain that he wasn't sure at all. That every step toward this plan felt like walking deeper into darkness.

But the alternative was staying where he was—hunting one at a time, watching Leira grow to hate him more each day, never having enough coin to escape.

One big score. Then he'd stop. He'd change.

He just had to survive one more night.

Ragar was waiting at his house, pacing the small porch like a caged animal. He spun when he heard Garik's footsteps.

'Well? How'd it go?'

'We're on.' Garik kept his voice flat, businesslike. Easier that way. 'Jeremiah's recruiting. We move tomorrow night.'

Ragar's face lit up with predatory excitement. 'Excellent! I knew you'd pull through, brother.'

*Brother.* The word hit differently now. Once it had meant something—family, loyalty, shared blood. Now it felt like a chain, binding him to choices he didn't want to make.

Garik leaned against the porch railing, needing the solid wood to ground him. 'Your job is Kian. We need enough Earthbind to lock down the village—prevent any transformations. And fifty vials of Wing-Bane to force-shift any we capture.' He'd done the math. Fifty vials meant fifty ravens. A devastating blow to their population.

Possibly an extinction-level event.

His stomach churned, but he kept talking. 'We load them in cages, get clear of the forest, then it's just transport and payment.'

Ragar's excitement dimmed slightly, replaced by calculation. 'That's a lot of potion, Garik. We're talking serious gold. Where are we getting that kind of coin upfront?'

'Tell Kian about the opportunity. If he wants more raven parts than he can count—enough to keep Volthar supplied for months—he'll extend the credit. This is an investment.'

'And if he says no?'

'He won't.' Garik pushed off from the railing. 'Kian's been complaining for weeks about not being able to meet Volthar's demands. We're offering him a solution. He'll jump at it.'

Ragar nodded slowly, his mind clearly working through the logistics. 'What about cages? We'll need something strong enough to hold them once they're shifted.'

'I have a man for that.' Garik had already thought it through—there was a blacksmith on the edge of town who owed him a favor and didn't ask questions. 'You focus on the potions. We need them by tomorrow afternoon.'

'Done.' Ragar clapped him on the shoulder, grinning. 'I knew this would work out. One big score, brother. After this, we're set for life.'

Set for life on blood money. On the corpses of families torn apart, children orphaned, an entire people driven closer to extinction.

But Garik just nodded. 'Get the potions. I'll handle the rest.'

As he walked away from Ragar's house, the night felt colder than it should. The stars overhead seemed to mock him—distant, untouchable, clean. Everything he wasn't.

Tomorrow night they'd raid the village.

Tomorrow night he'd become something worse than a hunter.

A monster.

But at least he'd be a monster with enough gold to stop being one.

The logic was circular, broken. He knew that.

He went anyway.

CAELEN

Dawn light filtered through the forest canopy in shafts of gold and green, painting everything with the promise of a new day. Caelen moved through the trees with practiced silence, his heart beating faster with each step toward Wyntown.

He hadn't slept. Had spent the night pacing his room, thinking about Tyrae's death, about the elders' continued inaction, about Leira.

Always about Leira.

She was the hunter's daughter. Enemy by blood. But she'd looked at him with those impossibly blue eyes and seen him as a person, not prey. Had shared her pain, her shame over what her father did. Had kissed him like he mattered.

And maybe—just maybe—she could help him stop this.

'Leira knows about the hunting,' he muttered to himself as he crossed into human territory. 'Her father talks to her, or around her at least. She might know when they're planning to strike next. Might know how to stop them.'

It was a thin justification for what he was really doing: going to see her again because he couldn't not see her. Because that brief kiss yesterday had burned itself into his memory like a brand.

Because he was fifteen and stupid and falling for someone he absolutely shouldn't be falling for.

The river came into view first, its surface catching the morning light. His stomach sank when he didn't see her there. The disappointment was physical, sharp in his chest.

Then he spotted her—blonde hair catching the sun like spun gold, pinned back with a leather strap. She was hanging laundry in the yard behind a small cottage, her movements efficient and practiced.

His heart lurched.

He started forward, then froze.

The cottage door opened. Garik stepped out onto the porch.

Caelen dove behind the corner of a nearby building, pressing himself flat against the rough wood. His pulse hammered in his ears so loud he was certain they'd hear it.

Garik surveyed the street with the casual alertness of a predator. Then he said something to Leira—too distant for Caelen to hear—adjusted his belt, and walked off in the opposite direction.

Caelen waited until the hunter disappeared around a corner, counting his heartbeats. One hundred. Two hundred.

Then he stepped out.

Leira had her back to him, reaching up to pin another sheet to the line. The morning sun lit her hair like a halo, made her look almost unreal.

He moved closer, trying to be quiet, but a twig snapped under his boot.

She spun, hand flying to her mouth. 'You nearly gave me a heart attack!'

But she was smiling. Actually smiling, her eyes bright with surprise and something else. Pleasure, maybe. Happiness at seeing him.

'Last thing I'd want,' Caelen said, grinning despite the danger of being here. 'Your heart's far too valuable for that.'

Her cheeks flushed pink. 'What are you doing here? If my father sees you—'

'Has he gone somewhere?' Caelen glanced toward where Garik had disappeared, keeping his voice casual.

Something like relief flickered across her face. 'Yes. He said something about business. Won't be back until tonight, probably.'

'Do you know where?'

She shrugged, finishing with the sheet. 'No idea. But it's hunting-related, I'm sure. Everything's always about hunting.' Bitterness crept into her voice. 'If he catches you here, Caelen, he'll kill you. He meant what he said at the bridge.'

'Then he'd better not catch me.' Caelen moved closer, emboldened by her smile, by the way she didn't step back. 'Besides, I'm very good at not being caught.'

'Are you?' Her eyebrow arched. 'You seem to have a talent for appearing exactly where you shouldn't be.'

'Maybe I'm exactly where I should be.'

The words came out more seriously than he'd intended. For a moment they just looked at each other, the morning air thick with everything unsaid.

Then Leira caught his hand, her fingers warm against his. 'Come on. Before someone sees.'

She led him through a maze of alleyways and back streets, moving with the confidence of someone who knew every hidden corner of this town. They ended up in an old barn by the river—abandoned, from the look of it, hay scattered across the floor and dust motes dancing in the light from gaps in the walls.

They collapsed into the hay, breathless and laughing, lying side by side staring up at the rafters.

'Are you a vagrant?' Leira asked, her tone half-teasing. 'Some wandering troublemaker looking for adventure?'

Caelen sputtered. 'A vagrant? Is that what you call every handsome, mysterious stranger who crosses your path?'

She laughed—that beautiful sound that made his chest feel too small. 'Alright, handsome stranger. Where do you really come from?'

The question hung between them. He wanted to tell her. Wanted to trust her with the truth.

But the truth was impossible. *I'm one of the people your father hunts. One of the ravens he kills for gold. And last night he murdered a woman named Tyrae while I stood in the village square demanding we fight back.*

'West,' he said finally. 'Small village. You wouldn't have heard of it.'

'Try me.'

'It's...' He scrambled for a name, any name. 'Millbrook. On the coast.'

She studied him with those sharp blue eyes, and he knew she didn't quite believe him. But she didn't push.

'What about you?' he asked, deflecting. 'Always lived here?'

'All my life. Born in that house, probably die in it too.' She said it lightly, but there was something sad underneath. 'Not much happens in Wyntown. Until you showed up.'

'Sorry about that. I tend to cause trouble.'

'I'm noticing.' But she was smiling again, close enough that he could smell the faint scent of lavender in her hair, see the exact blue of her eyes.

His heart was hammering again, but different now. Not fear. Something warmer.

'Leira—'

The barn door creaked.

They both froze.

'Damn it,' Leira hissed, grabbing his hand and pulling him to his feet. 'Farmer Mudwell. He checks the barn sometimes. Come on!'

They ran for a side door, hands clasped tight, trying not to laugh at the absurdity of it. As they reached the door, Leira turned back, rose on her toes, and pressed her lips to his.

It lasted only a heartbeat. Soft and quick and perfect.

Then she was gone, slipping out the main door with a last smile over her shoulder, leaving him standing there like an idiot with his heart trying to beat out of his chest.

Caelen waited until he heard old Mudwell's heavy footsteps fade, then slipped out the side door into the bright morning.

He was still reeling from that kiss—from the impossible reality of Leira, from the way she made everything else disappear—when he turned a corner and walked straight into Ragar.

'You again!'

The hunter's face twisted into a scowl, recognition and anger flashing across his features.

Before Caelen could react, Ragar's hand shot out and grabbed him by the scruff of his neck, yanking him forward with bruising force.

'Wait—what are you—let me go!' Caelen struggled, but Ragar's grip was iron.

'You've been sniffing around my niece, haven't ya, ya little weasel!' Ragar's breath was hot and sour in his face. 'Garik's gonna love hearing about this.'

Panic flooded through Caelen. His mind raced—he'd been so distracted by Leira, so caught up in impossible feelings, that he'd let his guard down. Let himself be vulnerable.

Stupid. So incredibly stupid.

Ragar dragged him through the streets, his grip never loosening despite Caelen's attempts to twist free. The morning sun beat down mercilessly. Sweat ran down Caelen's back.

And beneath them, his shadow.

The shadow that was too long, too angular, that shifted wrong when he moved. The shadow that would give him away if anyone looked closely.

*Please,* he prayed. *Please don't look down. Please don't notice.*

But Ragar's eyes were fixed ahead, his face set in grim satisfaction.

Their destination was a shed on the outskirts of town—old, weathered, its door secured with heavy chains. Ragar unlocked them with one hand while keeping his iron grip on Caelen with the other.

'Make yourself comfortable, lad,' Ragar said, his smile cruel. 'Garik'll be along to deal with you soon enough.'

He threw Caelen inside with brutal efficiency.

Caelen hit the ground hard, rolling across rough hay into a corner. The stench of old animal waste and rot filled his nose. He scrambled up, lunged for the door—

It slammed shut with a metallic clang.

The click of the chains being secured sounded like a death sentence.

'Enjoy your stay!' Ragar's laugh was muffled through the wood.

Then silence.

Caelen stood in the dim space, his heart hammering. A single small window high on one wall let in bars of dusty light, but it was too narrow to squeeze through.

He was trapped.

In a hunter's shed.

Waiting for Garik—the man who'd killed Tyrae last night, who was planning gods-knew-what next—to come deal with him.

The irony would have been funny if it weren't so terrifying.

Caelen sank down against the wall, his mind racing. He had to escape. Had to get back to the village before nightfall. Had to warn them—about what, he didn't know, but his instincts screamed that something was coming.

The hunters were planning something big. He'd heard it in the tavern, seen it in Garik's expression.

And he was trapped here, helpless, while whatever it was unfolded.

He looked up at the window, at the bars of light painting the floor.

The sun was still rising. He had time.

He had to have time.

Because if he didn't escape, if Garik discovered what he was...

Caelen pushed the thought away and started examining the shed's walls, looking for any weakness, any way out.

He would escape.

He had to.

Leira's face flashed through his mind—her smile, her kiss, the trust in her eyes when she'd taken his hand.

She didn't know what her father was. What Caelen was. The impossible chasm between them.

But maybe that didn't matter.

Maybe—

The sound of footsteps outside froze his thoughts.

Someone was coming.

Caelen pressed himself into the corner, barely breathing, and waited.

# CHAPTER SEVEN

*The Race*

The sun's warmth faded as dusk crept across Wyntown, shadows lengthening like grasping fingers. Inside the shed, Caelen pressed against the rough wooden wall, searching for any weakness in the weathered boards.

Nothing. The structure was old but solid enough to hold him.

Hours had passed since Ragar threw him in here. Hours of testing every plank, every nail, every corner of his prison. The shed was old, yes, but solid enough to hold him captive. The single barred window was too small to squeeze through, the door chained from outside.

He was trapped.

Footsteps approached outside—heavy, deliberate. The chains rattled.

Caelen backed into the corner, his heart hammering. He knew those footsteps.

The door swung open. Garik stood silhouetted against the dying light, his expression unreadable in shadow.

'So,' the hunter said, stepping inside. 'The boy returns.'

His voice dripped with cruel satisfaction. As he moved closer, the last rays of sunlight caught his face—and Caelen saw something there that made his blood run cold. Not just anger. Not just the predatory focus of a hunter who'd caught prey.

Certainty. Like a man who'd already decided exactly what he was going to do.

Caelen forced himself to stand straight, to meet Garik's eyes. 'You can't hold me here!' His voice came out stronger than he felt. 'You have no right—'

'No right?' Garik laughed, a harsh sound. He leaned against the doorframe, blocking the only exit. 'Boy, I've got every right. You've been sniffing around my daughter. Filling her head with ideas. Causing problems.'

'I haven't done anything to her—'

'Haven't you?' Garik's eyes narrowed. 'She's been different since you showed up. More defiant. More willing to question me. That's your influence.'

Good, Caelen thought but didn't say. She should question you. Should see you for what you are.

'Lucky for you,' Garik continued, his tone shifting to something almost conversational, 'I have other important matters to attend to tonight. Can't waste time dealing with some vagrant boy.' He studied Caelen with the casual disdain of someone swatting a fly. 'Maybe if you stay in here for a couple of days, you'll have time to think things through. Consider whether pursuing my daughter is worth the trouble.'

A couple of days locked in this shed. No food. No water. Just time to 'think.'

'Either way,' Garik added, turning toward the door, 'by then, you won't be a pain in my arse anymore.'

The phrasing was odd. Did he mean Caelen would give up? Learn his lesson? Or was there something darker in that casual dismissal—like Garik planned to do something more permanent after his 'business' was handled?

Caelen's mind raced, but he had no context, no information. Just a growing sense of dread.

'Wait!' Caelen called out, not sure what he was going to say, just knowing he couldn't let this end here.

But Garik was already outside.

'Ragar!' the hunter called.

His brother appeared at the window, peering in with a cruel grin. 'Comfortable in there, boy?'

'Plenty of time to think,' Garik said. He looked back at Caelen one last time. 'About what really matters. About making better choices.'

Then they were gone, their footsteps fading into the evening. The chains rattled back into place with a sound like a death knell.

Caelen stood alone in the dimming shed, his mind racing. What did Garik mean by that? 'By then, you won't be a pain in my arse anymore.' Was it just a threat? Or was there something specific the hunter was planning?

He sank to the floor, testing the chains one more time. Solid. Unbreakable without tools he didn't have.

He was trapped, and he had no idea for how long.

Minutes passed. Then more.

The light outside faded to purple twilight.

Then—footsteps again. Lighter this time. Quick and uncertain.

A voice, barely above a whisper: 'Caelen? Can you hear me?'

Caelen tensed, backing into the corner, preparing himself for another confrontation with Garik or Ragar.

But the voice that came through the door was different. Softer. Frightened.

'Caelen? Can you hear me?'

His heart leapt. 'Leira?'

'Yes.' Her voice was thick with tears. 'I'm so sorry. I didn't know they'd—I never thought—'

'It's not your fault.' He pressed his ear against the rough wood, trying to catch every word. 'Leira, you need to go. If your father finds you here—'

'He's busy with some job,' she said quickly. 'He won't be back for a while. But Caelen, I heard them talking. Him and Uncle Ragar. They're planning something terrible.'

Caelen's pulse quickened. 'What did you hear?'

A pause. He could hear her breathing, uneven and scared.

'Leira?'

'I—' Her voice caught. 'Nothing. It's okay. I'll find a way to get you out.'

'Wait!' But he heard her footsteps moving away from the door, circling around the shed.

A moment later, her face appeared at the small barred window, pale in the gathering dusk.

Then she gasped.

Caelen's stomach dropped. He'd forgotten—in the dim light filtering through the window, his shadow stretched across the floor behind him, too long, too angular, the edges pulling into shapes no human shadow should hold. The raven tell. The thing that marked him as other, as prey, as something to be hunted.

She stumbled back from the window.

'Leira—' He moved toward the bars, hands raised. 'Please, let me explain—'

'You're...' She stared at him, her blue eyes wide with shock. 'You're one of them. You're Arvi.'

The word hung between them like a blade.

This was it. The moment she realized what he was. The moment she ran screaming for her father, for the hunters, for anyone who would kill the monster she'd been consorting with.

'Yes.' His voice came out hoarse. 'I'm Arvi. I'm one of the people your father hunts. I should have told you, but I was scared that if you knew—'

'Then what?' Her voice sharpened with hurt. 'That I'd turn you in? Report you to my father? Is that what you think of me?'

'No! Leira, no. I just—' He gripped the bars, the cold metal biting into his palms. 'We're hunted for existing. Killed for what we are. You have to understand, trusting anyone is...' He couldn't finish the sentence.

She was quiet for a long moment, her face shadowed and unreadable.

Then she stepped back to the window. 'This changes nothing,' she said firmly. 'Your secret is safe with me.'

Relief flooded through him so intensely his knees weakened. 'Leira—'

'We need to get you out of here,' she continued, her voice taking on a determined edge. 'Quickly. I'll find the key.'

'You'll be in danger,' he protested. 'If they find out you helped me—'

'I'm not afraid.' Her gaze locked with his through the bars, fierce and unwavering. 'They won't touch you. Not if I have anything to say about it.'

Before he could argue further, she turned and disappeared into the shadows.

'Leira!' he whispered urgently.

But she was gone.

Caelen sank back against the wall, his heart pounding. She knew. She knew what he was, and she was still helping him.

Maybe not all humans were monsters.

Maybe there was hope for something more than endless war.

He just had to survive long enough to find out.

Time crawled. Minutes felt like hours as Caelen paced the small shed, listening for any sound of Leira's return.

What if she'd been caught? What if Garik had come back early? What if she'd had second thoughts and decided to tell her father after all?

The doubts circled like carrion birds.

Then—footsteps. Quick and light.

'Caelen?' Leira's voice, breathless.

'I'm here!'

The sound of metal on metal. The chains rattling. Then a heavy thud as they fell away.

The door creaked open.

Leira stood there, keys clutched in her trembling hands, her face flushed from running.

Caelen was across the shed in two strides, pulling her into an embrace before conscious thought caught up. She melted against him, and for a moment they just held each other, breathing hard.

'I thought you weren't coming back,' he whispered into her hair. It smelled like lavender and smoke.

'I had to go to Uncle Ragar's house,' she said, her voice muffled against his shoulder. 'He keeps a spare set of keys there. I waited until he left and then—' She pulled back, her face grave. 'Caelen, there's something happening tonight.'

The words sent ice down his spine. 'What?'

'I try not to listen to my father's business,' she said quickly, the words tumbling out. 'I don't want to know the details of what he does. But I heard him talking to Uncle Ragar. They're planning something big. A massive capture. They have other hunters. Equipment. A cage on wheels.'

Caelen's blood went cold. 'Where? Where are they going?'

She hesitated, her eyes filling with tears. 'I—'

'Leira, please.' He gripped her arms, trying to keep the desperation from his voice and failing. 'I need to know. People will die if I don't warn them.'

She swallowed hard. 'The village. Caelora. They kept saying the name. And they had maps, and...' Her voice broke. 'Oh god, Caelen. They're going to attack your people.'

The world tilted.

Caelora. His village. His home.

His parents.

Everyone he'd ever known, about to be slaughtered or captured while he stood here, helpless, miles away.

'We have to warn them.' The words came out strangled. 'Leira, we have to—when? When are they going?'

'Tonight. Soon, I think. They were gathering at the bridge when I snuck away.'

*Tonight.*

No time. No time to plan, to prepare, to do anything but run and pray he wasn't too late.

'I'm coming with you,' Leira said, her jaw set.

'No. It's too dangerous—'

'I said I'm coming.' She grabbed his hand, her grip fierce. 'My father is about to murder your people. The least I can do is help you try to stop him.'

He wanted to argue. Wanted to keep her safe, away from the violence that was coming.

But there wasn't time.

'Follow me,' he said, and they ran.

They sprinted through the darkening streets of Wyntown, Leira leading him through alleys and back ways, avoiding the main roads where hunters might see them.

His mind raced faster than his feet. How long did they have? An hour? Less? How fast could the hunters move through the forest? How quickly could he get to the village and sound the alarm?

Would anyone listen to him after his challenge to Illdran? Or would they waste precious minutes arguing while the hunters crept closer?

'The bridge,' Leira gasped, pointing ahead.

They burst from the alley onto the main road. The bridge loomed ahead, its stone arch pale in the twilight.

Empty. Thank the gods, empty.

They didn't slow, their footsteps echoing on stone as they raced across.

Caelen risked a glance back at Wyntown—at the town where Leira had lived her whole life, where her father was gathering his hunters for slaughter.

She didn't look back. Just kept running, her hand tight in his.

On the far side of the bridge, the forest rose up to meet them—dark, welcoming, dangerous. Caelen's territory now. His home.

'This way!' He veered right, onto a path only visible if you knew what to look for. 'Stay close. The forest is safe for me, but for you—'

'I trust you,' she said simply.

The words hit harder than they should have. Trust. From a hunter's daughter. For a raven boy she'd known for less than a week.

It felt like a miracle.

It felt like a lie he didn't deserve.

They plunged into the trees, darkness swallowing them whole. Behind them, somewhere in Wyntown, Garik and his hunters were moving. Ahead, in Caelora, his people were settling in for the evening, unaware that death was coming for them.

And between the two, Caelen ran through the forest with a girl who shouldn't be helping him, racing against time and fate and the terrible choices of desperate men.

He just hoped they'd be fast enough.

GARIK

The sun was setting as Garik stood with Ragar at the designated meeting point near the bridge. Other hunters were gathering—rough men who asked few questions and expected good pay. Exactly what they needed.

The cage wagon stood to one side, its iron bars catching the dying light. It looked like something for transporting animals.

Which, Garik supposed, was exactly how they were treating the ravens.

*Not animals,* the voice in his head insisted. *People. You're planning to cage people.*

He pushed the thought away. Too late for doubts now. The plan was in motion.

'Ragar, you got everything?' he asked, his voice low.

Ragar nodded, patting his pack. 'Aye. Kian wasn't happy about the deferred payment—looked like he'd bit into a lemon—but he handed over the goods.'

'He'll be singing a different tune when we bring him tonight's haul,' Garik said, trying for confidence he didn't feel.

Ragar grunted agreement, his eyes scanning the assembling hunters. 'What about the boy? The one sniffing around Leira?'

Heat flashed through Garik's chest. 'After tonight, he won't be a problem. I'll make sure of it.'

A lie. He didn't know what he'd do with Caelen. Part of him wanted to just let the kid go—he seemed harmless enough, clearly infatuated with Leira. But Ragar expected action, expected protection of family.

So Garik would deal with it. Later. After the raid.

After everything changed.

The last of the hunters arrived, and Garik called them together. Someone lit a lantern, casting his shadow long and dark across the assembled men.

He unfurled the map he'd drawn—crude but functional, showing the approaches to Caelora.

'Here's how this works,' he began, his voice carrying authority he'd learned from his father. 'Harick, you and the wagon stay on the road. Hidden. Wait for my signal. We can't have you spooking them before we're ready.'

Harick—a big man with a scarred face—nodded grimly.

'Three men approach from the north.' Garik pointed to the map, then to three hunters in the crowd. 'You, you, and you. Three more from the west—you three. Ragar, Jeremiah, and I take the south.'

The men murmured understanding.

'Once you reach the village, stay hidden. Spread out. When you hear my signal, you throw Earthbind onto the main paths. The stuff covers a wide area—makes a good loud pop when it goes off, which should draw them out to investigate.' He paused, making sure they understood. 'The Earthbind will prevent transformation, but the window is short. Maybe five minutes. We have to move fast.'

'What's the signal, boss?' someone called out.

Garik hadn't thought of that. 'An owl's hoot. Like this—' He attempted the call, but it came out strangled and ridiculous.

The men laughed, tension breaking.

'You'll know it when you hear it,' Garik said with a grin that felt like a mask. 'After the Earthbind, we move in. Herd them to the village center. Force Wing-Bane down their throats. Once they're shifted, they go in the cages. We load up, get out, come back here for sorting and payment.'

'What if they fight?' someone asked.

'Then you subdue them. But don't kill them.' Garik's voice hardened. 'Dead ravens are worthless. We need them alive to shift them. Anyone who kills one answers to me. Understood?'

Nods all around.

'Any other questions?'

Silence. The men were ready. Eager, even. The promise of gold making them bold.

'Then let's move out,' Garik said. 'And let's get rich.'

The hunters dispersed to their positions, voices low and excited. The wagon creaked as Harick urged the horse forward, moving to his hiding spot on the road.

Garik stood for a moment, watching them go. Ragar and Jeremiah waited nearby, checking their gear.

This was it. The point of no return.

He thought of Leira, probably at home right now, maybe wondering where he'd gone. Would she be proud when he came back with enough gold to give her a better life? Or would she look at him with those knowing eyes and see him for what he was?

A monster.

He'd become exactly what she accused him of being. Someone who could look at people and see only profit.

But it was too late to stop now.

The hunters were moving. The plan was in motion.

All that remained was to see it through.

Garik adjusted his pack, checked his weapons one last time, and headed into the forest with Ragar and Jeremiah.

Toward Caelora.

Toward the biggest payday of his life.

Toward the moment that would define what kind of man he truly was.

The forest swallowed them in darkness, and Garik didn't look back.

# CHAPTER EIGHT

*The Race Against Time*

The forest breathed around them as Caelen and Leira ran through the darkness. Ancient trees rose like sentinels, their branches whispering secrets as old as the earth itself. Somewhere ahead, hidden in the labyrinth of trunks and shadows, lay Caelora.

His home.

And Garik's target.

Caelen's lungs burned. His legs screamed for rest. But he pushed harder, Leira's hand tight in his as they crashed through undergrowth, stumbling over roots in the darkness.

'How much further?' Leira gasped beside him.

'Not far. Maybe another—'

A thunderous crack split the night.

They both froze, the sound echoing through the trees like a physical blow. It came from ahead. From the direction of the village.

'No,' Caelen breathed. 'No, no, no—'

Another crack. Then another. A strange blue glow began to seep through the forest canopy, painting the leaves in unnatural light.

Earthbind.

They were too late.

'We have to move faster!' Caelen broke into a sprint, abandoning caution for speed. Behind him, he could hear Leira's labored breathing, her footsteps struggling to keep pace.

The village came into view through a haze of blue fog—that cursed mist that trapped his people in their human forms, made them vulnerable, made them prey.

And through that fog, Caelen saw his nightmare made real.

Villagers stumbled from their homes, confusion and terror written on their faces. Some tried to shift, reaching for the change that would save them—wings, feathers, escape. But the Earthbind held them fast, trapping them in fragile human bodies.

'Why can't they transform?' The question came out strangled.

Leira's voice was hollow beside him. 'The fog. It must be preventing it somehow.'

Caelen's hands clenched into fists. He'd warned them. Had stood in the village square and begged them to prepare, to fight, to do *something*. And Illdran had dismissed him as an insolent child.

Now they were paying the price.

'I have to help them.' He started forward, but Leira's grip on his arm stopped him.

'Wait. Look.'

She pointed through the trees.

Garik and Ragar emerged from the forest's edge, leading a squad of armed hunters. They moved with the confidence of predators who'd already won, advancing on the helpless villagers like wolves circling wounded deer.

Caelen's blood turned to ice as he watched his people being herded together. He could see faces he knew—Tarron the baker, Luthais the butcher, Illdran with his weathered face twisted in fear.

And there, in the center of the terrified crowd, his parents.

His mother's hand clutched his father's arm. His father stood rigid, trying to shield her with his body. Both of them scanning the crowd desperately—looking for him, Caelen realized with a sick lurch. Looking for their son who wasn't there.

From the shadows, Caelen and Leira watched as Illdran stepped forward, his voice carrying across the square.

'Please, sirs. You don't have to do this. We mean you no harm. Just let us—'

A hunter's fist caught him across the face, sending the old raven stumbling backward.

'Shut it!' The hunter's laugh was cruel, echoed by his companions.

Rage flooded through Caelen, hot and consuming. His muscles tensed, preparing to charge, to fight, to do *something*—

Then a cart emerged from the mist.

It rolled forward with grinding inevitability, its lanterns casting monstrous shadows that danced across the blue fog. And mounted on that cart, illuminated by flickering light, was a cage.

Iron bars. Heavy locks. Large enough to hold dozens of people.

Large enough to hold everyone Caelen loved.

The cart's wheels creaked as it stopped in the village center. One of the hunters pulled open the cage door with a metallic screech that made Caelen's teeth ache.

But they didn't start loading people yet.

Instead, the hunters pulled out vials—dozens of them, glinting in the lantern light. Wing-Bane. The potion that forced the transformation whether the raven wanted it or not.

'Hold them steady!' one hunter barked.

What followed was systematic brutality. The hunters grabbed villagers one by one, forcing their jaws open, pouring the Wing-Bane down their throats while they struggled and choked.

Caelen watched in horror as Tarron convulsed, his body jerking as the potion took hold. Bones cracked and reformed. Flesh compressed. In seconds, the baker who'd always saved sweet rolls for the children became a black-feathered bird, squawking in distress as rough hands grabbed him.

One by one, they forced the transformation. One by one, they threw the ravens into the cage like sacks of grain.

His mother fought when they grabbed her, twisting in their grip. His father tried to shield her, but a hunter's fist caught him in the stomach. He doubled over, and they poured the Wing-Bane down his throat.

Caelen had to bite his own hand to keep from crying out as he watched his father's body shrink and shift, black feathers bursting from skin.

The hunter tossed him into the cage. His mother followed moments later, her raven form small and trembling.

The forced transformations continued—each one accompanied by the wet sounds of bones reshaping, the flutter of emerging feathers, the distressed cries of ravens who couldn't understand what had happened to them.

When the last villager had been transformed and thrown into the cage, the hunter slammed the door shut. The lock clicked with terrible finality.

Inside the iron bars, dozens of ravens fluttered and called, confused and terrified, pressed together in a mass of black feathers.

Garik's laugh cut through the silence—harsh and grating, a sound that scraped against Caelen's soul.

'Looks like a full house!' The hunter's voice rang with triumph.

Beside him, Leira trembled. Her fingers clenched and unclenched at her sides. Her eyes were wide, unblinking, fixed on the scene before them.

On her father, laughing as he caged innocent people like animals.

Caelen saw the exact moment something broke inside her. Saw the last thread of hope—that maybe her father wasn't truly a monster, that maybe there was some justification she'd missed—finally snap.

A sound to their left made them both turn.

A figure emerged from the shadows—naked, as all ravens were after transformation. Lamruil, the village shopkeeper, a man Caelen had known since childhood.

Leira immediately averted her gaze, her cheeks flushing even in the dire circumstances.

'Caelen.' Lamruil's voice was grim. 'I knew you'd show up. Didn't expect company though.' His eyes flicked to Leira, assessing, suspicious.

'She's with me,' Caelen said firmly. 'She helped me escape. Warned me about the raid.'

'She's a *hunter*—'

'She's on our side.' Caelen's tone left no room for argument. 'Now tell me—how many got away?'

Lamruil's expression shifted from suspicion to something like hope. 'A dozen, maybe more. We scattered when the Earthbind hit. Some of us slipped into the forest before they could round everyone up.'

'Good.' Caelen's mind raced, assembling a plan from fragments of desperation and fury. 'Find them. Bring them here. We need everyone we can get.'

'What are you planning?'

'A rescue. A fight. Whatever it takes.' Caelen met Lamruil's eyes. 'We're not letting them take our people.'

Lamruil studied him for a long moment, then nodded. His form blurred, shifted, became a raven in a burst of feathers. He launched into the trees without another word.

Minutes ticked by with agonizing slowness. Then figures began to emerge from the forest—naked, shivering, frightened, but free. They gathered in the shadows, a ragged assembly of those who'd escaped the cage.

Caelen counted them. Fourteen. Against how many hunters? He'd seen at least ten, maybe more.

Not good odds. But better than nothing.

'Listen to me.' He kept his voice low, aware of the hunters still searching the village. 'We need a diversion. Something to draw them away from the cage, split their forces. If we can get them into the forest, away from the Earthbind fog, we'll have the advantage.'

'How?' someone whispered.

'We lead them on a chase. Transform, show ourselves, make them pursue. But stay away from that blue fog—the moment you enter it, you're trapped.'

He saw understanding dawn on their faces. Fear too, but also determination.

'Spread out,' Caelen ordered. 'Pick your moments. Draw them deep into the trees, then lose them in the darkness. Make them think there are more of us than there are. Create chaos.'

One by one, they melted back into the shadows.

Caelen turned to Leira. Her face was pale but set with determination.

'Are you ready?' he asked quietly.

'Absolutely.' No hesitation. No doubt.

They'd been prey long enough.

Now it was time to become something else.

## EARLIER THAT EVENING - GARIK

The wagon's iron-clad wheels groaned against the wooden planks of Bearwater Bridge, the sound echoing across the river below. Garik led his band of hunters into the forest's waiting darkness, the fractured moonlight barely penetrating the canopy above.

Ten men. One wagon. Enough Earthbind and Wing-Bane to subdue an entire village.

This was it. The raid that would make them rich or get them killed.

'Once we hit the forest, we go silent,' Garik said, his voice carrying down the line. 'Stick to the plan. We can't afford to alert them before we're in position.'

Murmurs of agreement rippled through the group. Garik glanced at Ragar, walking beside him.

'Second thoughts, brother?' Ragar asked, reading his expression.

'Just wondering if the cage is big enough.' A deflection. The truth was more complicated—a churning in his gut that might have been anticipation or might have been guilt.

*They're not people,* he told himself for the thousandth time. *Just ravens. Just animals wearing human shape.*

The lie felt thinner every time he repeated it.

Ragar chuckled. 'We'll make it work. Always do.'

They plunged deeper into the forest. Garik ordered the torches doused once they were clear of the bridge—stealth mattered now. The men moved with surprising quiet for their size, years of hunting making them careful with their footfalls.

'From here, Ragar, Jeremiah, and I go ahead,' Garik said when they reached the fork in the path. 'The rest of you wait for my signal at the village outskirts. When you hear it, throw the Earthbind and move in fast. Understood?'

Nods all around.

Garik, Ragar, and Jeremiah broke away from the main group, disappearing into the trees. The forest at night was a different beast entirely—shadows within shadows, every sound amplified, every movement magnified by imagination.

'You sure we're going the right way?' Jeremiah asked after they'd been walking for twenty minutes.

'Of course.' Garik tried to sound confident. Truth was, the forest all looked the same in the dark. He was navigating by memory and instinct, neither of which felt particularly reliable at the moment.

'You've stopped to check the stars three times,' Jeremiah observed. 'That confused look suggests otherwise.'

Garik bit back a sharp retort. 'I know where we're going.'

'If you say so.' Jeremiah stroked his beard, unconvinced.

They walked in tense silence, broken only by the occasional rustle of nocturnal creatures. Every snap of a twig made Garik's hand move toward his weapon. Every shadow could be a raven scout. Every moment they spent lost in these trees was a moment for their plan to fall apart.

Then, through a gap in the trees ahead—light. The warm glow of lanterns and hearth fires.

'We've arrived,' Garik breathed.

They crept to the edge of the tree line. Below them, nestled in a clearing, Caelora spread out like a collection of children's toys. The structures were more sophisticated than Garik had expected—woven wood and living trees shaped into dwellings, connected by paths of packed earth and smooth stone.

It looked... peaceful. Beautiful, even.

*Like a place people would call home,* the traitorous voice in his head whispered.

'Spread out along this stretch,' Garik ordered, pushing the thought away. 'When I give the signal—the owl hoot—you throw your Earth-bind onto the main paths. But only on my signal. We need them all outside before we close the trap.'

Ragar and Jeremiah melted into position, leaving Garik alone at his vantage point.

He watched the village. Watched ravens in human form moving through the streets, going about their evening routines. A woman—pregnant, he realized with a jolt—stepping out to empty a basin of water. An old man sitting on his porch, smoking a pipe and watching the stars. Children playing some kind of game with stones near a well.

*Not animals,* his conscience screamed. *People. Families. Lives you're about to destroy.*

But he'd come too far to turn back now.

A rumble in the distance made him smile despite himself. Harick and the wagon, right on schedule. The sound would draw curious villagers out to investigate.

Everything was falling into place.

Garik drew a breath, cupped his hands around his mouth, and let out an owl's hoot that was, admittedly, pretty terrible.

But it worked.

Blue light exploded across the village outskirts as the hunters threw their Earthbind. The bottles shattered with satisfying pops, releasing that cursed fog that would trap the ravens in their human forms.

Screams erupted from the village. Doors flew open. Ravens stumbled out, confusion and terror on their faces, reaching desperately for transformations that wouldn't come.

Garik stood and walked into the chaos, his men emerging from the trees like a pack of wolves.

'Round them up!' he shouted. 'Quickly, before the Earthbind wears off!'

His hunters moved with brutal efficiency, herding the trapped ravens toward the village center. Some of the birds managed to escape into the sky before the fog took hold—Garik watched them disappear into the night with a flash of relief he didn't want to examine.

Better that some got away. Better that this wasn't total slaughter.

Ragar appeared at his side. 'Plan's working perfectly.'

'A few escaped.'

'Can't catch them all.' Ragar didn't seem bothered. 'We've got plenty.'

They reached the village square. The cage wagon rolled into view, its arrival greeted by fresh screams from the captives.

Garik surveyed the crowd they'd gathered. More than he'd expected. Many more.

An old man—one of their elders, by his bearing—stepped forward. 'Please, sirs. You don't have to do this. We mean you no harm. Just let us—'

One of Garik's men punched him in the face. The old man went down hard.

'Shut it!' the hunter laughed.

Garik should have stopped it. Should have said something about unnecessary violence.

He didn't.

The cage door opened with a metallic screech.

The Arvi shuffled forward, hollow-eyed with shock and fear. One by on they were forced to drink the wing-bane potion, transforming them instantly. Garik watched them file into the cage—families clutching each other, children crying, old ones struggling to climb the high step.

One woman caught his eye as she was shoved toward the cage. Middle-aged, dark-haired, terror etched on her face. She looked... familiar somehow.

Then he realized why.

She looked like Tyrae. The woman he'd killed two nights ago. Same build. Same features. Maybe a sister? A cousin?

Maybe the husband who'd chased them through the forest was somewhere in this crowd, being loaded into a cage because Garik had already murdered his wife.

The cage door slammed shut. The lock clicked.

Garik heard himself laugh—a harsh sound that felt disconnected from his body. 'Looks like a full house!'

The words tasted like poison.

'Oi!' One of his men called out. 'There's a naked woman out there!'

Garik's attention snapped toward the trees. A figure—definitely human-shaped, definitely female—was visible at the edge of the blue fog.

Bait. Obviously bait.

Some of the ravens had escaped. Now they were trying to draw his hunters away from the cage.

Smart.

'Get her!' Garik ordered, playing along. Let his men chase shadows in the forest. The real prize was already secured.

Half his hunters took off toward the trees, eager for more captures.

Garik turned back to the cage, to the frightened birds, within.

And for just a moment—one terrible, crystalline moment—he saw Leira's face among them.

Not really. His daughter was safe at home, unaware of what her father had become.

But he could imagine her there, trapped and terrified, looking at him with those accusing blue eyes.

*Is this who you want to be?*

He shook his head, clearing the vision.

Too late for doubts. Too late for conscience.

The job was done. The village was broken. All that remained was loading the cage and collecting payment.

Garik turned away from the accusing eyes and began kicking in doors, checking for stragglers.

The night was far from over.

# CHAPTER NINE

*The Price of Freedom*

Caelen's heart hammered against his ribs as he crouched in the shadows near the cage. Around him, the fourteen who'd escaped the initial raid waited for his signal, their naked forms trembling in the cold night air.

*This isn't just about me,* he reminded himself. *It's about all of us.*

The weight of their trust pressed down on his shoulders like a physical thing. These people—his people—were counting on him to save their families. Their friends. Their lives.

'Now,' he whispered.

They moved like ghosts through the village, slipping between houses, using the darkness as cover. The blue Earthbind fog had mostly dissipated, but the hunters still prowled the streets, searching for stragglers.

Caelen and Leira reached the cage first. Inside, dozens of ravens fluttered and called in distress, their black feathers catching the lantern light. Some pressed against the bars, recognizing Caelen, their eyes almost human in their desperation.

He pressed a finger to his lips, signaling for silence.

The cage had a heavy padlock securing the door. Caelen pulled out the piece of wire he'd been carrying, hands moving with practiced speed as he worked the lock.

Nothing. The mechanism was too complex, too well-made.

'Damn it,' he hissed. 'We need the key.'

Leira's hand touched his shoulder. 'I'll find it. The hunters must have—'

Heavy footsteps. Close. Too close.

They both froze as a figure rounded the corner of a nearby house. Ragar.

His eyes widened when he saw Leira, then narrowed with fury when he spotted Caelen.

'What are you doing out here, Leira?' His voice was rough with confusion and anger. 'You're supposed to be back in town.' His gaze snapped to Caelen. 'You! How did you—'

Leira moved.

Her knee drove into Ragar's groin with brutal efficiency. The big man doubled over with a grunt of pain, and in that moment of vulnerability, Leira's hands moved to his belt, snatching the ring of keys hanging there.

She tried to run, but Ragar's arm shot out, catching her ankle. She went down hard, the keys flying from her hand.

'Leira!' Caelen lunged forward.

'Go!' She threw the keys toward him, her voice desperate. 'Caelen, now! We're out of time!'

More footsteps. More voices. The other hunters, drawn by the commotion.

And Garik, emerging from between two houses, his face a mask of rage and incomprehension as he took in the scene—his daughter on the ground, his brother clutching his groin, and Caelen scrambling for the keys.

'Stop him!' Garik roared, charging forward.

Caelen's fingers closed around the keys. He sprinted for the cage, Garik's footsteps thundering behind him. His hands shook as he jammed key after key into the lock, each failed attempt making his heart sink lower.

Third key. Fourth. Fifth—

Click.

The lock sprang open. Garik was getting close. But Caelen didn't throw the cage door wide. Not here, surrounded by hunters. Not when they were still vulnerable. He had to get moving.

'Hold on!' he called to the ravens inside in their language. 'I'm getting you out of here!'

He left the cage closed—unlocked but secured—and sprinted for the front of the wagon.

Garik's hand caught Caelen's shoulder, spinning him around. 'You little—'

A raven dove from above—one of the fourteen who'd escaped earlier—talons raking across Garik's face. The hunter stumbled back with a curse, blood streaming from fresh wounds.

More ravens descended, attacking the hunters who'd gathered, creating chaos and confusion. The escapees were fighting back, protecting Caelen, buying him precious seconds.

Caelen didn't waste them. He vaulted into the driver's seat, grabbed the reins, and snapped them hard. The horse bolted forward, the cage rattling behind them, its occupants squawking in alarm at the sudden movement.

A glance back showed him Leira, still on the ground, surrounded by hunters. Garik was pulling her to her feet, his face twisted with fury and something that might have been pain.

Their eyes met across the distance. Hers were filled with determination and something else—acceptance, maybe. Or goodbye.

'Go!' she mouthed.

Then they were around a corner, and she was gone from sight.

Caelen's chest constricted. Every instinct screamed at him to turn back, to fight, to save her. But the cage behind him was still full of his people—still locked as ravens, still trapped, still vulnerable.

He had to get them to safety. To somewhere he could free them properly.

*I'll come back for you,* he promised silently. *I swear it.*

The forest swallowed them whole as they raced away from Caelora, the sound of pursuit fading behind them.

A rustling from the cage behind him made Caelen glance back. Through the bars, he could see the ravens stirring, some beginning to shift back to human form as the Wing-Bane finally wore off.

His mother's face appeared at the bars—human again, tears streaking her cheeks, her hands gripping the iron.

'Caelen,' she called out, her voice raw.

'I know, Mother.' He kept his eyes on the road, his hands tight on the reins. 'We're almost there. Almost safe.'

'You're safe now, Mother.' He tried to smile back at her, even though she couldn't see his face from her position in the cage. 'All of you.'

'Because of you.' Her voice carried over the rattling of the wagon. 'And because of that girl. The hunter's daughter.'

Caelen's throat tightened. 'Leira.'

'She saved us.'

'And I left her behind.'

'You saved your people.' His mother's voice was firm, even from behind the bars. 'You did what you had to do. What she wanted you to do.'

But it didn't feel like enough.

The wagon creaked through the forest, following paths Caelen knew by instinct more than sight. He was heading for Silenthollow—a small settlement on the edge of Fae territory. Neutral ground. Safe ground.

If they could just make it there before the hunters caught up.

Behind him, in the cage, more ravens were shifting back to human form as the Wing-Bane wore off. He could hear voices now—confused, frightened, asking questions he couldn't answer while keeping the horse moving.

They'd lost their village. Their homes. Everything they'd built.

But they were alive.

That had to count for something.

Silenthollow appeared through the trees not as a clearing but as a seamless extension of the forest itself. Structures rose from dark timber, curved to follow roots rather than defy them, their surfaces softened by moss that seemed to grow by design rather than neglect. Paths wound between dwellings in natural contours, as though the settlement had always been there, waiting to be discovered rather than built.

Figures emerged from the structures—small in stature, wiry, moving with a contained grace that made Caelen think of predators conserving energy. Fae. Not the glittering courtly spirits of children's tales, but something older. Quieter. Closer to root than crown.

They wore garments of bark fiber and undyed cloth, their hair thick and tangled with bits of twig and dried blossoms. But it was their eyes that made Caelen's breath catch—bright, unblinking, deeply appraising. Assessing him. The wagon. The cage full of desperate ravens.

Weighing everything before deciding whether to speak.

Then another figure stepped forward, and Caelen's exhaustion-fogged mind struggled to process what he was seeing.

She was human. Unmistakably so. But she moved through the Fae like water through reeds, with an unhurried certainty that made it seem as though time adjusted itself to her pace. Tall where the Fae were small, her dark hair falling in loose waves to mid-back, catching the green-gold light that filtered through the canopy. She wore flowing fabrics of deep blue and muted ivory that whispered at her ankles when she walked, the cloth moving around her as though the air itself settled more neatly in her presence.

Lady Armina.

The legendary warden of Arghost. Protector of the border between mortal and Fae lands.

Her face held a quiet warmth—high cheekbones softening into a calm, measured expression. But it was her eyes that arrested him. Clear blue, steady, unnervingly perceptive. When her gaze met his, Caelen felt less observed and more understood. Not judged. Not forgiven. Simply known.

It was deeply unsettling.

Caelen pulled the horse to a stop, his arms aching from gripping the reins. His whole body trembled with exhaustion and adrenaline crash.

'Forgive our intrusion, milady.' He kept his voice respectful, aware of dozens of Fae eyes still watching, still assessing. 'We were attacked. We seek sanctuary.'

Lady Armina's expression didn't change, but something in the quality of her attention sharpened. She spoke—not loudly, but with a gentle cadence that made Caelen lean forward without realizing he'd done so.

'Attacked?' Her voice carried an accent he couldn't quite place, soothing without being soft. 'By whom?'

'Hunters from Wyntown.' Caelen fumbled with the cage lock, his hands shaking. 'They used Earthbind and Wing-Bane. Caged us. We barely escaped.'

The lock clicked open. Caelen swung the cage door wide.

His people began to emerge—some still in raven form, others human and desperately trying to cover themselves with whatever they could find. Naked. Traumatized. Afraid.

The Fae watched in continued silence, their bright eyes taking in every detail. Lady Armina's gaze swept across the refugees, and Caelen saw something flicker in those clear blue eyes. Not pity. Something deeper. Recognition, perhaps, of a violence she'd seen before.

When she spoke again, her voice was lower. Quieter. And somehow, everyone leaned closer to hear it.

'You poor souls.'

She turned to the Fae, speaking in whispers that sounded like wind through leaves. But where the Fae had been still and assessing, at her words they moved as one, their earlier watchfulness transforming into purposeful action.

Some disappeared into dwellings and returned with blankets woven from bark fiber and soft grasses. Others brought water, food, simple things offered without cere mony but with clear intent. They didn't fuss. Didn't crowd. Just provided what was needed with the same quiet efficiency they brought to everything else.

Lady Armina moved among the refugees with that same unhurried certainty, her presence somehow soothing despite speaking no platitudes. When she paused beside an elderly woman still shaking with shock, she simply placed a hand on her shoulder—and the woman's breathing steadied.

There is power in her, Caelen realized. But not the loud, crackling kind. It rested in stillness. In patience. In the way even the firelight from nearby dwellings seemed to bend around her without swallowing her shadow.

She felt less like a ruler of the forest and more like one of its deeper roots. Ancient. Anchored. Watching.

'You will be safe here,' she said, her voice carrying to all the refugees without rising. 'The forest protects its own.'

A hand on Caelen's shoulder made him turn. Illdran stood there, a blanket wrapped around his shoulders, looking older than Caelen had ever seen him. His face was bruised from the hunter's blow, one eye swollen nearly shut.

'I owe you an apology, lad,' the elder said quietly.

The words Caelen had wanted to hear for so long. But now, standing in this strange place among these strange people, having left Leira behind with the hunters, they felt hollow.

'Yes,' he said flatly. 'You do. We could have prevented this. If you'd listened. If you'd let us prepare—'

'I know.' Illdran's voice was heavy with regret. 'I thought I was protecting our people by keeping them from war. Instead, I left them defenseless. That blood is on my hands.'

Caelen wanted to rage at him. To list every life lost, every person caged, every moment of terror that could have been avoided.

But he was too tired. And Illdran already knew.

The Fae had withdrawn to a respectful distance, still watching but no longer assessing. They'd made their decision. The ravens were under their protection now.

'We'll do better,' Illdran said. 'I promise you that. No more waiting. No more hiding.'

'Good.' Caelen turned away, done with the conversation.

His parents were waiting nearby, both wrapped in Fae blankets that smelled of earth and growing things. His father's arm was around his mother's shoulders. When they saw him, they moved forward as one, pulling him into an embrace.

'We're so proud of you,' his father murmured into his hair.

Caelen let himself sink into their warmth for just a moment, breathing in the familiar scent of them. Then he pulled back, his mind already racing ahead.

'I have to go back,' he said.

His mother's hand tightened on his arm. 'What? No, Caelen—'

'Leira's still there. She helped us escape. Gave up everything to save us. I can't just leave her with those hunters.'

'She's one of them,' someone nearby muttered. 'A hunter's daughter. She made her choice.'

Caelen spun toward the voice, anger flaring hot in his chest. 'She made the right choice. And now she's in danger because of it. I'm going back for her.'

His father studied his face for a long moment, then nodded slowly. 'The horse is spent, but there's one in the Fae stables that might serve. I'll speak with Lady Armina.'

'Thank you.'

Around them, the Fae continued their quiet work—tending to the wounded, offering shelter to the displaced, asking nothing in return. This was not charity born of pity. It was something older. Deeper.

The forest protecting its own.

And right now, Leira was alone in that forest, surrounded by men who saw her as currency or worse.

Caelen had saved his people.

Now he had to save her.

Or die trying.

LEIRA

Garik's fingers dug into Leira's arm hard enough to bruise, his grip like iron shackles. His eyes blazed with a fury she'd never seen before—not just anger, but betrayal. Hurt.

Around them, the hunters muttered and cursed, their voices rising in a dangerous crescendo. They'd lost their prize. Lost their payday. And they were looking for someone to blame.

'What have you done?' Garik's voice was barely controlled, each word clipped and harsh. 'Do you understand what you've done?!'

Leira swallowed hard but said nothing. What could she say? That she'd chosen right over family? That she couldn't stand by while innocent people were caged and sold?

That she'd rather die than become what he'd become?

'Where's our gold, Garik?' one of the hunters demanded. 'We risked our necks for this raid, and now we've got nothing!'

'Your gold is safe,' Garik said, not taking his eyes off Leira. 'I'll handle this.'

'They've escaped! Because of her!' A burly hunter stepped forward, hand on his sword. 'Maybe we should take our payment from her instead.'

The threat in his words was unmistakable. Leira's heart hammered, but she lifted her chin, meeting his gaze with as much defiance as she could muster.

'No one,' Garik's voice cut through the growing hostility like a blade, 'touches her. Understood?'

For a moment, the square fell silent.

Then Ragar, still clutching his groin and breathing hard, pushed himself upright. 'Brother's right. We'll get the gold. One way or another.'

'Your brat cost us a fortune,' the scarred hunter spat. 'She should pay for it.'

'I said no.' Garik's hand moved to his weapon. 'Anyone who wants to argue can take it up with me.'

The hunters subsided, muttering, but Leira could feel their eyes on her—calculating, angry, dangerous.

Garik looked at Jeremiah, who stood off to the side watching the whole scene with an unreadable expression.

'We should move,' Garik said to Ragar. 'Before they decide to take matters into their own hands.'

Ragar nodded. They began to walk, Garik pulling Leira along, Ragar limping beside them.

'Not so fast.'

The voice came from behind them. Then a wet, choking sound.

Leira spun to see Ragar staring down at the blade protruding from his stomach, his face a mask of shock and incomprehension.

'No!' The scream tore from her throat.

Ragar crumpled to the ground, blood pooling beneath him.

Garik froze, his face draining of color. For a moment, he just stared at his brother's body. Then his eyes snapped to Leira.

'Run!' he shouted, releasing her arm and shoving her toward the forest. 'Run!'

Leira ran.

Behind her, she heard shouting, the ring of steel, chaos erupting as the hunters turned on each other in the aftermath of Ragar's murder.

She plunged into the forest, branches tearing at her clothes and skin, her breath coming in ragged gasps.

Heavy footsteps crashed through the undergrowth behind her. Multiple hunters, their voices raised in pursuit.

A explosion of wings erupted from the canopy above. Ravens—the ones who'd escaped earlier—dove at her pursuers, talons and beaks striking at vulnerable faces and hands.

Screams. Curses. The hunters fell back, trying to defend themselves.

Leira kept running, using the distraction to put more distance between herself and her pursuers.

Behind her, through the chaos, she heard her father's voice.

'Keep running, Leira! Don't stop!'

She risked a glance back and saw him, surrounded by ravens, blood streaming from a dozen small wounds. He was holding them off, keeping them from pursuing her.

Buying her time.

Then a hunter broke through the swarm, blade raised, and drove it into Garik's back.

Leira's hand flew to her mouth, stifling the scream that threatened to give away her position.

Her father dropped to his knees, the hunter pulling the blade free and raising it for another strike.

'Find the girl!' someone shouted.

The ravens attacked again, a black storm of fury and feathers, giving Leira the precious seconds she needed to run deeper into the forest.

She ran until her lungs burned. Until her legs gave out. Until she collapsed against a tree, sobs tearing from her throat.

Her father was dead. Murdered by his own men—men he'd trusted, worked with, called brothers.

The price of greed. The price of trafficking in stolen lives.

But also the price of trying to protect her at the end.

Leira pressed her face into her hands and wept for the father she'd lost twice—once to monstrosity, and now to death.

Dawn was just beginning to lighten the sky when a hand clamped down on her arm, yanking her to her feet.

'Well, hello there, Leira.'

Jeremiah. His grin was cold and calculating, his grip bruising.

'Let me go!' She twisted, trying to break free.

'The way I see it,' he said, his eyes raking over her in a way that made her skin crawl, 'you owe me quite a sum of gold, lass.' His grin widened. 'And I plan on collecting. One way or another.'

Leira's blood turned to ice.

She'd escaped the cage.

But she wasn't free yet.

# CHAPTER TEN

### The Rescue

The horse's breath came in ragged gasps beneath Caelen as dawn light filtered through the trees. Every hoofbeat carried him closer to Caelora, closer to answers, closer to Leira.

He'd left Silenthollow before anyone could argue. Lady Armina had arranged for a fresh mount—one of the Fae's own horses, small but tireless—and his father had pressed a knife into his hand with a look that said everything words couldn't.

*Be careful. Come back alive.*

The wagon tracks were easy to follow in reverse, the deep ruts carved by iron wheels leading him back through the forest like a trail of breadcrumbs. As morning brightened, the trees began to thin, and Caelora came into view.

Or what was left of it.

Caelen slowed the horse to a walk, his stomach churning at the sight. The village wasn't destroyed—the structures still stood, the paths remained—but it felt hollow. Empty. Like a body with the soul ripped out.

Figures moved between the houses. Ravens who'd escaped the initial capture, slowly returning from their hiding places in the woods. Caelen recognized some of them—Neia the healer, Corvath the blacksmith's apprentice, others whose names he knew but couldn't recall through the fog of exhaustion.

They looked as haunted as the village felt.

He dismounted, his legs nearly buckling after the hard ride. 'Leira,' he called out, his voice hoarse. 'Have you seen a human girl? Blonde hair, blue eyes. She was with me during the escape.'

Blank stares. Confused expressions.

'The hunter's daughter,' he clarified, desperation creeping into his voice. 'She helped us. She was here when the hunters—where did she go?'

Neia stepped forward, her face drawn with weariness. 'Caelen. Thank the forest you're alive. But I haven't seen any human girl. After you left with the wagon, there was...' She paused, choosing her words carefully. 'Violence. Among the hunters themselves. They turned on each other.'

Caelen's blood ran cold. 'What happened?'

'One of them—the big one, Ragar—was killed. Stabbed by his own men. Then the one called Garik fought the others. He was trying to protect someone, I think, but there were too many. The birds helped where they could, but...' She shook her head. 'It was chaos. When it was over, most of the hunters fled. Some were dead. Garik among them.'

Garik. Dead.

Caelen waited for the surge of satisfaction, the vindication of seeing Leira's father—Jonah's killer—brought down.

It didn't come. Just a hollow ache and a more pressing terror.

'The girl,' he pressed. 'Did you see where she went?'

'There was a girl running into the forest,' Corvath offered. 'Blonde, like you said. But I don't know what happened to her after. The fighting was too fierce.'

She'd run. Escaped. But to where?

'Wait!' Neia called as Caelen swung back onto his horse. 'Where are the others? The ones who were caged—are they safe?'

'Silenthollow,' Caelen said over his shoulder. 'With the Fae. Lady Armina has them.'

He didn't wait to see their reactions. Just kicked the horse into motion, heading for the one place Leira might have gone.

Home.

Wyntown was quieter than Caelen had ever seen it. The streets felt wrong—too still, too empty, like everyone had decided to stay indoors. The aftermath of the failed raid, maybe. Hunters who'd returned without their prize, spreading word of the disaster.

Or maybe they just sensed something bad was coming.

Caelen kept to the shadows as much as possible, acutely aware of how his shadow fell wrong, how any direct sunlight would give him away. Midday was approaching—the worst possible time for this.

But he couldn't wait.

Leira's house stood near the edge of town, small and weathered. Caelen had only seen it from a distance before. Now he approached the door with his heart hammering, aware this could be a trap, could be suicide.

He didn't care.

He tried the latch. Unlocked. He pushed the door open and stepped inside.

Empty.

The single room was neat but abandoned. A cold hearth. Un-washed dishes on the table. A woman's shawl draped over a chair—Leira's, probably. Everything spoke of people who'd left in a hurry or simply never come home.

Of course Garik wasn't here. He was dead in Caelora.

And Leira... where was Leira?

Caelen moved through the small space, searching for any sign, any clue. But there was nothing. Just the quiet emptiness of a house that had lost its occupants.

He stood in the center of the room, frustration and fear warring in his chest.

If Leira hadn't come home, where would she go?

Caelen stood in the street, his mind racing. She'd been running from hunters. From her father's former allies. Men who blamed her for losing their prize.

Men who might want payment in other ways.

The thought made his stomach turn.

He needed information. Needed to ask questions without drawing attention to himself.

The bridge. There was always someone at the bridge.

Caelen found an old man sitting on a bench near the approach, pipe smoke curling lazily into the air. He was watching the tavern up the hill, where sounds of shouting and rough laughter spilled into the street.

'Excuse me,' Caelen said, keeping his voice polite. Unthreatening. 'I'm looking for someone. A young girl—blonde hair, blue eyes, about sixteen. Did you see anyone like that pass by this morning?'

The old man's gaze swung from his pipe to Caelen, and something knowing flickered in his eyes. 'You're one of them, ain't you? One of the Raven Clan.'

Caelen's hand moved instinctively toward the knife his father had given him. 'I don't know what you—'

'Your shadow, lad.' The old man gestured with his pipe. 'Gives you away clear as day. Shame, the way they treat your kind in this town.'

You be careful. There are men here who'd kill you without a second thought.'

For a moment, Caelen considered running. But the old man's tone wasn't hostile. Just... weary. Knowing.

'I'm looking for a girl,' Caelen repeated. 'A human girl. Please. It's important.'

'Aye, I saw her.' The old man took a long pull from his pipe. 'This morning. Looked like Garik's daughter, now that you mention it. But she was with Jeremiah. Odd pair, that. She didn't look happy about it.'

Jeremiah.

Ice flooded Caelen's veins. 'Where did they go?'

'Jeremiah's place, over the ridge.' The old man pointed with his pipe. 'He came back to town later, went into that tavern. Been there ever since, from the sound of it.'

Caelen was already moving. 'Which way? Where's his house?'

The old man gave directions—up the road, past the bend, a small cottage set back from the path.

'Thank you,' Caelen called over his shoulder, breaking into a run.

Behind him, the old man's voice followed: 'Be careful, lad. Jeremiah's not a good man.'

Caelen knew. Gods, he knew.

The image of Leira trapped with that hunter, alone, helpless—it made his vision narrow, made his hands shake with more than exhaustion.

He mounted his horse and urged it into a gallop, the ridge rising ahead like a wall he'd break through or die trying.

## LEIRA

The room was barely larger than a closet. Leira sat on the floor, her back against the wall, trying to control her breathing.

Panic wouldn't help. Fear wouldn't help.

She needed to think.

'Now you make yourself comfortable, lass,' Jeremiah had said, his grin making her skin crawl. 'I've got some business to attend to. Then I'll be back and we can get better acquainted.'

His wink had been the worst part. Like this was all some kind of game.

The door had locked from the outside. She'd already tried it—tested the latch, thrown her weight against the wood. Solid. Too solid.

The window was small, set high in the wall. Too high to reach without something to stand on. Even if she could reach it, it was barely large enough to squeeze through.

She looked around the room. Old rags in one corner. A few crates, half-rotted. Nothing that could help her break down the door.

But maybe she could reach the window.

Leira dragged the largest crate beneath the window, tested its stability with her weight. It creaked but held. She climbed up, her hands finding the windowsill.

The glass was dirty but intact. And beyond it—forest. Trees. Escape.

If she could just break through.

Leira climbed down and grabbed one of the crate's wooden slats, pulling until it splintered free. The wood bit into her palms, but she ignored the pain.

Back on the crate. She swung the plank at the window.

The glass cracked but didn't break.

Again. Harder this time.

The window shattered, fragments falling like sharp rain. Leira used the plank to clear away the remaining shards from the frame, then leaned out as far as she dared.

'Help!' Her voice came out hoarse. 'Someone help me!'

The forest swallowed her cry. Nothing moved in the trees.

Leira kept calling anyway, her throat growing raw, her voice breaking.

Then—hoofbeats.

A rider appeared through the trees, moving fast. Too fast to be casual. Someone searching.

'Help!' Leira screamed. 'Up here! Please!'

The rider pulled up short beneath the window. Looked up.

Caelen.

Relief hit her so hard she nearly fell from the crate. His face—exhausted, streaked with dirt, his eyes red-rimmed—was the most beautiful thing she'd ever seen.

'Leira.' His voice cracked on her name. 'Are you hurt?'

'I'm locked in. Jeremiah—he locked me in here and—'

'I'll get you out.' He reached up through the window, and she grabbed his hand, held it like an anchor. 'I promise. But you need to let go so I can find a way in.'

She nodded, forcing herself to release his hand.

'I'll be right back,' he said. 'I promise.'

Then he was gone from sight.

Leira climbed down from the crate, her whole body shaking. He came. He actually came back for her.

Sounds from elsewhere in the house—glass breaking, wood splintering, Caelen's grunts of effort. He was trying to get in through another entrance.

Then heavy thuds against her door. An axe, she realized. He'd found an axe.

Each blow sent splinters flying. Each impact made hope surge brighter.

The door gave way with a final crack, and Caelen burst through, axe still in hand, his eyes wild.

Leira ran to him. He dropped the axe and caught her, and for a moment they just held each other, breathing hard, alive.

'Are you hurt?' he whispered against her hair. 'Did he—'

'No. I'm okay. I'm okay now.'

She was crying. Hadn't realized she was crying until she felt the tears on her cheeks, the sobs shaking her shoulders.

Caelen's arms tightened around her. 'We need to go. Before he comes back—'

'Well, well.' The voice came from behind Caelen, cold and amused. 'The prodigal hero returns.'

Jeremiah stood in the doorway, a sword in his hand, his grin sharp as the blade.

'I was wondering if you'd show up, bird-boy. Saved me the trouble of hunting you down.'

Caelen pushed Leira behind him, his hand moving to the knife at his belt.

It seemed very small compared to Jeremiah's sword.

'Let her go,' Caelen said, his voice steady despite the tremor in his hands. 'Your fight is with me, not her.'

'Oh, I don't know about that.' Jeremiah's eyes flicked to Leira. 'The girl owes me quite a bit of gold. Figured I'd take payment one way or another.'

The implication made Leira's skin crawl.

'She doesn't owe you anything,' Caelen said.

'No? Her father and uncle are dead because of you birds. My payday gone. Someone's got to pay for that.'

Jeremiah advanced into the room, sword raised.

Caelen moved to meet him, knife ready.

And Leira realized with terrible clarity that if this fight happened, Caelen would die.

She had to do something.

But what?

# CHAPTER ELEVEN

*Darkness Rising*

Caelen positioned himself between Leira and Jeremiah The blue fog from the shattered Earthbind vial was already seeping across the floor, reaching for him with invisible fingers.

He felt it the moment it touched his skin—a coldness that sank deep into his bones, locking something vital inside him. The transformation. He couldn't shift. Couldn't escape as a raven even if he wanted to.

Grounded.

'Keep back, Jeremiah,' Caelen said, his voice steadier than he felt.

Jeremiah's grin widened. 'Oh, I don't think so, boy.' He pulled another vial from his coat—Wing-Bane, the liquid inside catching the light. 'The night wasn't entirely wasted after all. One beak is better than none, wouldn't you say?'

He was going to force the transformation. Trap Caelen in raven form, helpless and small.

Then kill him.

Leira's hand gripped Caelen's shoulder from behind, her fingers tight with fear.

Jeremiah lunged.

Not with the sword—that would have been cleaner, quicker. Instead, he dropped his weapon and went for Caelen's throat with one hand, the vial raised in the other.

'Time to hold still, bird-boy!'

Caelen twisted away, but the room was too small, the space too confined. Jeremiah's weight crashed into him, sending them both sprawling. Leira hit the wall hard, crying out.

The impact drove the air from Caelen's lungs. Jeremiah's knee drove into his chest, pinning him. His vision started to gray at the edges as Jeremiah's hand closed around his throat.

'Open up,' Jeremiah snarled, forcing the vial toward Caelen's mouth.

Caelen bucked, twisted, tried to throw him off. But Jeremiah was heavier, stronger, and the Earthbind had stolen his only advantage. He couldn't shift. Couldn't escape.

The vial's rim touched his lips—

A wet, meaty thunk.

Jeremiah's body went rigid. His eyes widened, mouth opening in a soundless gasp. The vial slipped from his fingers, shattering on the floor.

He toppled sideways, revealing Leira standing behind him, the axe still raised, her face white with shock and determination.

The blade had buried itself in Jeremiah's back. Blood spread across his shirt in a dark stain.

He tried to speak, tried to move, but only managed a wet gurgle. Then his eyes went glassy, and he was still.

Leira dropped the axe like it had burned her. Her hands were shaking. Her whole body was shaking.

'Leira—' Caelen gasped, trying to sit up.

She rushed forward, helping to roll Jeremiah's body off him. Caelen sucked in great gulps of air, his throat aching where Jeremiah had gripped it.

'Are you hurt?' Leira's voice was high, strained. 'Did he—'

'I'm okay.' Caelen grabbed her hand, holding tight. 'You saved me. Leira, you—'

'I killed him.' The words came out flat, shocked. 'I killed him.'

'He was going to kill me.' Caelen pulled himself to his feet, still holding her hand. 'You did what you had to do.'

She looked down at Jeremiah's body, at the blood pooling beneath him. Her face was very pale.

'We need to leave,' Caelen said gently. 'Before someone comes. Before—'

She nodded, still staring at the body.

Caelen pulled her away, toward the door, away from the dead hunter and the blue fog still lingering in the room.

Outside, the fresh air hit them like a blessing. Leira bent double, breathing hard, her hands on her knees.

'I've never—' She stopped, swallowed. 'I've never killed anyone before.'

'I know.' Caelen put his hand on her back, feeling her trembling. 'I know. But Leira, you saved my life. Do you understand? Without you, I'd be dead right now.'

She straightened slowly, her eyes finding his. They were bright with unshed tears but steady. Determined.

'I couldn't let him hurt you,' she said simply.

The weight of those words—the choice she'd made, the line she'd crossed to save him—hit Caelen like a physical blow.

'Leira, I—' He struggled to find words big enough for what he felt. 'When I thought I'd lost you, when you were here and I was at Silenthollow, my heart felt... empty. Like something vital had been torn out.'

Her hand came up to touch his face, her fingers gentle against his cheek. 'I love you,' she whispered. 'I know it's fast, I know we barely know each other, but Caelen—I love you.'

'I love you too.' The words came easily, truthfully. 'You mean everything to me.'

They kissed then, desperate and fierce, alive against all odds.

When they finally pulled apart, both breathing hard, Caelen managed a shaky smile. 'We should go. Get you somewhere safe.'

'Home?' Leira asked, her voice small.

Home. The empty house where her dead father would never return. Where she'd have to figure out what came next, alone.

'Yes,' Caelen said. 'And then... we'll figure out the rest. Together.'

The walk back to Leira's house was quiet. They moved through Wyntown's empty streets like ghosts, both lost in their own thoughts.

When they reached the small cottage, Leira paused at the door, her hand on the latch.

'I need to tell you something,' she said. 'My mother... she died when I was born. It's just been my father and me. And now—' Her voice broke. 'Now it's just me.'

Caelen's heart ached for her. 'You're not alone. I promise you that.'

She managed a weak smile, then pushed the door open.

The house was as empty as when Caelen had searched it earlier. Cold. Silent. Waiting.

'I have to go back to my village,' Caelen said, hating the words even as he spoke them. 'Make sure everyone's safe. Help them rebuild. But Leira—I'll come back. As soon as I can. I swear it.'

She nodded, blinking back tears. 'I know. Just... be careful. Please.'

He pulled her into one more embrace, breathing in the scent of her hair, memorizing the feel of her in his arms.

'I will. And you—you'll be alright here?'

'I'll manage.' She stepped back, squaring her shoulders. 'I always do.'

He believed her. This girl who'd killed to save him, who'd given up everything to do what was right—she was stronger than she knew.

Caelen forced himself to walk to the door. To step outside. To leave her standing alone in that empty house.

It was one of the hardest things he'd ever done.

As he rode away into the gathering dusk, he looked back once. Leira stood in the doorway, watching him go.

He would come back. He had to.

SILENTHOLLOW

Twilight painted the sky in shades of purple and gold as Caelen rode into Silenthollow. The Fae settlement was bustling with activity—his people preparing to leave, gathering belongings, loading wooden wagons that the Fae had provided.

Going home. Or what was left of home.

His father spotted him first, relief flooding his weathered face. 'Caelen. Thank the forest. Did you find her?'

'I found her.' Caelen dismounted, his body aching from too many hours in the saddle. 'She's safe. Back in Wyntown.'

'Good.' His father gripped his shoulder. 'I'm glad. That girl... she saved us. We owe her a debt.'

Caelen nodded, unable to speak past the tightness in his throat.

The Fae had arranged for drivers—stone-faced, gruff individuals who clearly weren't thrilled about the assignment but would see it through. The wagons were simple but sturdy, enough to carry the refugees and what few possessions they'd managed to save.

'Caelen.'

He turned to find Lady Armina approaching, moving with that same unhurried grace that made everything around her seem to slow down.

'A word, if I may?'

'Of course, milady.' He followed her a short distance from the crowd, to where they could speak privately.

Her clear blue eyes studied him with that unnerving perception. 'Your courage has not gone unnoticed. What you did—freeing your people, returning for the girl—it speaks well of your character.'

'I only did what was necessary.'

'Necessity and courage are not mutually exclusive.' She paused, and something shifted in her expression. Something darker. 'I must warn you, Caelen. A storm is coming. Darkness gathering on the horizon.'

A chill ran down his spine despite the warm evening air. 'What do you mean?'

'The hunters who attacked your people were not acting alone. They serve a darker power.' Her voice lowered, and Caelen found himself leaning in to hear. 'A magika named Volthar. Ancient. Powerful. Corrupt beyond measure.'

The name sent ice through Caelen's veins. He'd heard it before—in the tavern, when the hunters spoke of their employer. When Illdran's face had gone pale at the mention.

'You know of him,' Lady Armina observed. Not a question. A statement.

'I've heard the name,' Caelen admitted. 'The hunters mentioned him. Said he was paying them for... for us.'

'Then you understand the danger.' Her expression was grave. 'What you have done—freeing his prizes, killing his hunters—will not go unanswered. Volthar does not forget debts owed. Nor does he forgive those who cost him what he seeks.'

Caelen's blood ran cold. 'He'll come for us.'

'Perhaps. Perhaps not immediately. But he will not forget.' Her hand touched his arm, light as a falling leaf. 'Be watchful. Protect your people. And know that the Fae will remember the debt we owe you. Should you need sanctuary again, our doors remain open.'

'Thank you, milady.'

She smiled, and it transformed her face into something almost otherworldly in its beauty. 'Go. Your people need you. And Caelen—' She paused. 'That girl. Leira. Hold onto her. Love like that is rare in this dark world.'

Then she was gone, gliding away between the trees like morning mist.

Caelen stood for a moment, her words echoing in his mind.

*A storm is coming.*

He shook off the premonition and returned to his people. They needed to get home. Needed to start rebuilding.

Whatever storm was coming, they would face it together.

The village felt different when they returned.

Not just empty—though it was that too, with so many homes abandoned, so much damage from the raid. But there was a new energy in the air. A determination Caelen had never seen before.

Illdran had changed. The elder who'd counseled patience and hiding was gone, replaced by someone harder. Grimmer. Realistic.

Wooden ramparts were rising around the village perimeter. Training grounds had been cleared where before there'd been gardens. The sound of swords clashing in practice echoed through the trees.

They were preparing for war.

'We won't be caught unprepared again,' Illdran said when Caelen found him overseeing the construction. 'You were right, lad. About all of it. We can't just hide and hope anymore.'

It was vindicating to hear. But it also made Caelen's stomach turn. Because preparing for war meant accepting that war was coming.

He threw himself into the work—helping rebuild damaged homes, training with the others, learning to fight properly instead of just defending himself. The days blurred together in a haze of exhaustion and purpose.

But his thoughts kept drifting to Leira. Was she safe? Was she managing alone in that empty house? Did she think of him the way he thought of her—constantly, achingly?

He wanted to go back. But the village needed him. His people needed him.

Soon, he told himself. As soon as things were stable, he'd go back to Wyntown. Back to her.

Three weeks after their return, a commotion at the village entrance drew Caelen from his work on the ramparts.

A crowd had gathered, villagers clustering together with worried expressions. Two guards stood at attention, their swords drawn, facing a cloaked figure that had appeared on the path.

Caelen pushed through the crowd, his hand moving instinctively to the knife at his belt.

The stranger was old—Caelen could see that much from the weathered skin visible beneath the hood. He carried a twisted staff, gnarled wood that seemed to pulse with a faint, sickly light.

'I said, what do you want here, stranger?' one of the guards demanded, his voice tight with tension.

The stranger's mouth twisted into something that might have been a smile. His teeth, what few remained, were black and rotting.

'So,' he said, his voice like gravel scraping over bone, 'you are the ones who killed my hunters.'

Ice flooded Caelen's veins.

'Who are you?' the guard asked, though Caelen already knew. Already felt it in his bones.

The stranger raised his staff, and the air around him seemed to darken, to curdle like spoiled milk.

'I am Volthar,' he said, and his voice carried across the crowd like thunder. 'Commander of legions. Envoy of the darkness. And you—' His smile widened, revealing that graveyard of teeth. 'You are mine to claim.'

He slammed the staff against the ground.

Fire erupted from its tip—not normal flames, but something darker, tinged with purple and green, spreading across the ground like living corruption.

'Run!' Caelen's voice cut through the moment of frozen horror. 'Everyone, run! Now!'

The crowd broke, scattering in all directions.

And Volthar's laughter followed them, echoing through Caelora like a promise of nightmares to come.

The storm Lady Armina had warned about?

It had arrived.

Dear reader,

I must take a moment to express my deepest gratitude to each one of you who journeyed with me through the enchanting realms of 'The Tales of The Sundering Twilight: Raven's Bane'. Your dedication to reaching the final page is not just a testament to your love for fantasy but also a beacon of encouragement that fuels my passion for storytelling.

Remember, the journey doesn't end here. There are many more stories to tell, more mysteries to unravel, and more adventures to embark upon in the world of Arghost. Stay tuned for the upcoming chapters, short stories, and the unfolding sagas that await.

In closing, I extend my heartfelt thanks for your unwavering support. Your engagement and love for the series make every word, every character, and every twist in the plot immensely fulfilling. Here's to more magical adventures and enchanted tales in the days to come!

I would really like to get to know you and thank you, so please sign up for my newsletter at **www.derrenparsonsauthor.com** and together, we'll venture into lands only accessible through the portals of visionary fiction. As a thanks, you'll gain access to exclusive giveaways, discounts, glimpses of works-in-progress, and a free ebook. And be sure to leave your own review on Amazon, Instagram, Goodreads, and TikTok to let us all know your opinion of Raven's Bane and The Tales of The Sundering Twilight series!

**Facebook**: AuthorDParsons **Instagram**: @derrenparsonsauthor **TikTok**: @derrenparsonsauth **GoodReads**: Derren Parsons

With a deep sense of gratitude,
Derren Parsons

# Appendix A : A Brief History of Trees

The story of the trees in Arghost is a truly epic tale, spanning millennia of survival, evolution, and adaptation. The Seekers of Knowledge, the esteemed scholars of Arghost, meticulously chronicled the journey of the majestic trees. Piecing together a vivid account of their struggles and triumphs.

As the powerful Athris, the one true light, formed the world, he imbued it with his own power to keep the darkness at bay. The world was initially a tumultuous place, buffeted by harsh and unforgiving climates that made survival near impossible.

But soon things changed. The weather ceased its endless volatility, becoming more stable, albeit still harsh. It allowed for some very hardy beings to appear.

The very first life in the world was the trees, enormous trees that reached the heavens. Covered in dense foliage that contrasted the bleak landscape that sustained them. They were the guardians of the land, bringing light to the world and hope for its future.

In a world battling to keep the darkness at bay, the trees were a guiding light. They would move around the land seeking the comfort of the most amiable climates in which to thrive and produce their offspring. Their movements, although slow, were deliberate, as it took a great deal of energy expenditure to move even one inch.

The "Great Migration", as it was later called, was a staple of the world for many millennia. The trees grew to large numbers. Soon, other flora appeared, filling the landscape with beauty beyond measure.

But soon was the age of the Cataclysm. The world broke apart, and some trees became separated from the herd, forced to exist in climates that weren't overly favorable. To survive, they evolved over many years, new species grew that were more tolerant.

As time went on, the trees became tired and longed for a stable home. Many stayed where they were and just gave up, losing the ability to walk, settling into areas, and becoming dormant. Whilst others grouped together. Although no longer moving, they kept their abilities by staying in groups. Working together to protect themselves from other dangers that had arisen in Arghost.

One such place is the Dewforrest in Cliodaven.

The Dewforrest is a place of wonder and awe, a testament to the resilience and adaptability of the trees of Arghost. It is a place of renewal and rebirth, where the cycle of life continues uninterrupted, and the beauty of nature shines through in all its glory. As the sun sets over the Dewforrest, casting a warm and golden glow over the land, one cannot help but be filled with a sense of peace and contentment. Knowing that the trees are still there, silently watching over the world and guiding it toward a brighter future.

# SNEAK PEAK

## TURN THE PAGE FOR A SNEAK PEEK OF

THE CHRONICLES OF ARGHOST VOLUME I
THE SECOND RISING

# THE SECOND RISING - THE CHRONICLES OF ARGHOST - CHAPTER 1

*The Hunt*

N iama's pulse hammered, blurring the forest's edges. Leaves whispered underfoot as she ran, breath tight, senses razor-sharp. Ahead, the elk crashed through brush with a sharp crack, flight frantic.

The elk was alone. It should have been with a herd—elk didn't range solo this deep into winter. But she'd seen no tracks, no droppings, nothing but this single animal.

The herds were gone. Not thinning. Gone.

'Keep up,' she hissed over her shoulder.

Coseo didn't answer. His ragged breath tore behind her—too loud.

Niama slowed, raising a clenched fist. They slid to a halt beneath alder and thorn. She dropped to one knee, palm to damp earth. Fresh. Warm. Close.

Wind shifted.

She cursed silently and angled left, downslope, keeping their scent away. Brambles clawed her calves, thorns biting leather. She ignored the sting. Hunger cut deeper.

She glanced back. Coseo's face had paled, sweat darkening his collar.

'Breathe.'

He nodded, jaw clamped, and followed.

They crept forward. Tawny hide flickered through trees. The elk burst into a small clearing and stopped, sides heaving, steam curling from its nostrils in the cold.

Niama sank lower, bow in hand. Too open. No escape but the far treeline. If it bolted, they'd lose it.

She nocked an arrow.

The elk lifted its head, ears twitching. Somewhere above, a bird burst from the branches. The animal froze.

Coseo shifted. A twig snapped. The elk lunged.

Later, Niama would remember this moment. How a single snapped twig nearly cost them everything. How sound carried in winter air.

She'd remember it when the screaming started in the dark.

Niama drew and released in one motion.

The arrow struck high, driving into muscle. The elk screamed, stumbled, crashed through brush, and collapsed in a spray of leaves and frost.

Silence pressed close, the forest holding its breath.

Her hands shook once—then stilled.

Coseo exhaled a shaky laugh. 'By the light...'

Niama was already moving—low, knife ready, eyes on the flank. Only when stillness settled, when she was certain the elk wouldn't rise again, did she relax.

'That was close.'

'You dropped it with one shot.' His eyes widened, fatigue forgotten for a moment. 'I didn't even see the opening.'

'You thought too loudly,' she cut in, a smile tugging her mouth.

She knelt beside the elk, hand to its neck. Warmth lingered beneath fur. She bowed her head, murmuring quiet thanks—old words for bark, root, and blood-soaked earth. This life would not be wasted.

Winter would ease, if only a little.

She rose, knife steady, and began the work.

The elk was smaller than it should be. Ribs showing. A winter kill—already weakened by hunger before her arrow found it. The meat would be lean, tough.

But it would feed the village for two days. Maybe three if they stretched it.

Two days, she thought. Then what?

Coseo stared, chest still heaving. 'Another breath and we'd have lost it.'

Niama allowed a brief smile, a quick nod—thanks enough. He'd remember the shot. She'd remember the wait.

'Apologies. Leg fell asleep.' He winced, shifting weight.

Niama glanced back, red hair slipping loose. 'Patience was never your virtue, Cos.' She glanced at the blood on his hands, the dirt under his nails. 'We both smell like death now.'

She rested a hand on the flank one last time, feeling warmth ebb. 'We'll get you home,' she murmured to the creature. 'To the hunger waiting beyond the trees. To the children with hollow cheeks.'

Coseo nodded, humor gone, and helped shoulder the load.

She wiped her blade clean and wondered—not for the first time—what would happen when the forest no longer answered her prayers.

The journey home was quiet, the elk's weight heavy between them.

Mistwood lay deep in the Erbour Forest, trees close and old, ground remembering every footstep. It was the heart of Illadrel's southern reaches, bark and stone shaped together, nothing apart from the forest that birthed it.

Niama felt the change as the path wound deeper into familiar territory. Air thickened with damp moss, sap, loam crushed under leather. Branches bent aside in silence. Roots rose where feet expected them. The forest knew them here.

This was elven land, shaped by long familiarity.

Niama had grown beneath these boughs, learned to read the forest as others read script. Yet her bond was forged, not born. She remembered nothing before the day they found her bleeding among ferns, past stripped clean as bark from a fallen tree. The elders never spoke of it. Their silences clung tighter than answers.

Tonight, those questions could wait. The village needed meat, not mysteries.

Dusk crept in. Birds settled. Insects stirred. The sun slipped behind the Orborus Mountains, staining the canopy ash and amber.

Mistwood emerged, alive with motion. Torches flickered around the ancient heart tree, flames darting like fireflies among roots. Voices overlapped. Laughter rang.

'That's new,' Coseo murmured.

Too many voices. Niama slowed as they neared the village center. Bodies pressed everywhere—more than she'd seen outside of harvest festivals. Firelight danced across unfamiliar faces.

A villager pushed through the crowd, grin wide. 'Triumphant hunt?'

Niama shifted her grip on the elk, suddenly aware of how small it was. How little it would feed them. 'Hard-won. What's happening?'

'Summons from the elders. Every settlement sent word. Representatives too.' The villager's smile dimmed. 'We feast while we wait for news from the north.'

News from the north. Niama's stomach tightened.
Nothing good ever came from the north.

# THE SECOND RISING - THE CHRONICLES OF ARGHOST - CHAPTER 2

*The Gathering*

They entered the crowd, and the feast swallowed them whole.

Smoke curled thick, carrying roasting flesh and sap-rich wood. Drums pulsed beneath flutes' bright trills, the rhythm thrumming through the earth, felt more than heard. Bodies pressed close—villagers from Mistwood mingling with unfamiliar faces, representatives from settlements Niama had only heard named in passing.

The bonfire roared at the center, flames leaping high enough to paint the lowest branches gold. Faces glowed in the firelight, eyes bright, smiles unguarded. Children darted between adults' legs, shrieking with laughter. Sparks drifted upward like wandering stars, disappearing into the canopy's darkness.

Someone pressed a strip of meat into Niama's hands. She bit down. Juice ran hot, rich and smoky, herbs sharp beneath the char. It tasted of effort, blood, cold earth—survival earned. She closed her eyes briefly, letting the noise blur into warmth, the fear of the empty forest fade beneath the press of living bodies.

'The day has been bountiful,' Uthru said beside her.

She turned. The elder watched with quiet approval. 'You've done the village proud, Niama.'

She inclined her head. 'Fortune favored us. Herds thin each season.'

Uthru's smile faded. Lines deepened around his mouth, his eyes. 'Our troubles run deeper than hunger.' He glanced toward the heart tree where other elders were gathering in the shadows, their faces grave. 'Tonight we speak of matters that cannot wait. Enjoy the warmth while it lasts.'

He squeezed her shoulder once—a gesture that felt like both comfort and warning—then moved away, his form swallowed by the crowd.

Niama watched him go, unease settling cold in her stomach despite the fire's heat.

Coseo appeared at her elbow, chewing. 'What was that about?'

'I don't know.' She wiped grease from her fingers. 'But I don't think we're going to like it.'

Around them, the feast continued. Drums quickened. Someone began a song—voices rising, harmonizing, the old words about spring and plenty that felt hollow in her mouth. She didn't join in.

The forest beyond the firelight seemed to press closer, listening.

The horn's call cut through the feast, long and resonant, pulling night taut.

Conversations stuttered. Laughter died. The drums fell silent mid-beat.

Niama set aside her food and followed Coseo toward the circle. Others were already moving, faces shifting from celebration to wariness. Children were ushered toward the outer edges. Hunters moved forward, settling onto logs and stones arranged in concentric rings around the heart tree.

The elders sat on worn benches beneath the ancient trunk, their backs to bark that had witnessed centuries. Firelight flickered across weathered faces—Uthru at the center, Gretha to his left, old Torven to his right. Rolana stood behind them, a hunter herself, arms crossed.

Niama found a place near the front, Coseo beside her. Bodies pressed close on all sides. The air felt heavy, expectant.

Uthru stood.

'We must speak of matters that cannot wait.'

Silence fell like a blade.

Niama's hand found Coseo's shoulder as someone jostled her from behind. His muscles were tense beneath her palm.

'Dire tidings from the north,' Uthru continued, his voice carrying across the gathering. 'Aesulyn villages burn.'

Niama's chest tightened. Aesulyn. She had met the Namite—desert dwellers of Aesulyn—last spring. Three families, maybe four. Children who'd gathered around her bow, asking how far arrows could fly.

'Homes ruined. Survivors taken south, into Ghija's iron mines under Ijovar.'

She saw it behind her eyes—thatch catching, children screaming, the smell of burning flesh and green wood. Her fingers dug into her palms hard enough to hurt.

Uthru's gaze swept the circle. 'Some claim Ijovar's hand guides these acts. Others whisper of darker agents.' He paused. The fire crackled in the silence. 'Sightings of actari.'

A murmur rippled through the gathering like wind through grass.

A woman near the edge backed away, hand flying to her mouth. The hunter beside Niama went rigid, leather creaking as his fists clenched. Coseo's breathing quickened, shallow and tight.

Lhoris of Riverbreak barked a laugh—too loud, too sharp in the quiet. 'Actari? Children's tales. Ghosts to frighten fools from wandering at night.'

Niama shifted, boots grinding into earth. She'd grown on those stories—blood-soaked shadows with eyes like coals, creatures that served ancient darkness and showed no mercy. Her mother—no, not her mother, the woman who'd raised her—had whispered them as warnings when Niama ranged too far as a child.

Voices rose around her. Some nodded agreement with Lhoris, faces set with determination to believe in mundane threats. Others shouted him down, fear bright in their eyes.

Gretha rose from her bench, slowly, her white braid catching firelight. The arguments died.

'They are real,' she said, voice calm but unyielding as stone. 'Legends endure because they were born of truth. The actari serve the darkness between stars. Where they walk, nothing remains untouched. Nothing remains alive.'

Lhoris turned away sharply, jaw clenched. 'We face hunger, not phantoms. Our stores thin. The prey vanishes. The forest itself falters. These are the enemies we know.'

'And if they share a cause?' Uthru asked quietly.

'On whose word?' Lhoris demanded, wheeling back. 'Whose testimony do we trust with our lives?'

'Balen and his son,' Uthru said. 'Traders we've known twenty years. Men who've never lied about the roads they've walked.'

'A convenient story from men seeking shelter and food.'

Uthru's jaw tightened, a muscle jumping in his cheek. 'We will not dismiss warning because it frightens us. That way lies death.'

Gretha's voice cut through before Lhoris could respond. 'If true, it could mark the Second Rising. Darkness does not return without purpose. It does not wake without hunger.'

The name struck like a dropped blade—the Second Rising. Whispers ran through the crowd. Someone sobbed once, quickly stifled.

Firelight twisted across the elders' faces, shadows tangling as if alive, as if something moved just beyond the flames' reach.

Niama swallowed hard. The world felt brittle, like ice over deep water. One wrong step and everything would crack.

Uthru raised his hands, calling for silence. The gesture was slow, weary. 'Enough. Let us not jump to conclusions when we lack knowledge. We will seek counsel first.' His eyes lifted past the gathering, toward the forest's depths. 'From the Seer of Washrock Rise.'

A stir ran through the circle—part fear, part something darker. Washrock Rise. Niama had heard the name in whispers. A place where paths shifted. Where hunters went and didn't return.

Rolana stepped forward from behind the elders' bench, her scarred hands visible in the firelight. She'd survived a bear attack in her youth; everyone knew the story. Now her face was grim.

'There's more the council must hear,' she said. 'Hunters found tracks deep in the forest. Not made by any beast we know.'

The murmurs died. Every eye fixed on Rolana.

'Three weeks past, beyond the northern ridge. Two weeks ago, near Greymire Pond.' She paused, her gaze sweeping across the hunters in the front rows. 'A week ago, near the old cairn.'

Niama's blood went cold.

*The old cairn. Where they found me.*

Her vision narrowed. Sound became distant, muffled. The old cairn—the place she'd been drawn to three days ago, compelled by something she couldn't name. The place where her life had begun, her memory empty as a scraped bowl.

Uthru's gaze found hers across the fire. Not surprise in his eyes. Confirmation. Recognition.

He'd known. He'd known and waited to see if she'd felt it too.

'Five days ago,' Rolana continued, her voice steady despite the tension crackling through the crowd, 'the eastern watch found tracks a half-day's walk from here. Whatever made them is circling Mistwood. The pattern is deliberate. Tightening.'

The circle went utterly silent. Even the fire seemed to quiet, flames lowering as if cowering.

'We have days,' Rolana said. 'Not weeks.'

Another hunter stood—Maren, young but respected—his voice shaking. 'I found a deer yesterday. Near the eastern border. It wouldn't run.' He swallowed hard. 'Just stood there shaking, eyes wide and white. Like it had forgotten how to fear wolves because something worse was behind it. I... I left it there. Couldn't bring myself to kill something already dead inside.'

The silence that followed was suffocating.

Niama's hands trembled. She clenched them, nails biting into her palms. *Searching*, Rolana had said. *Deliberately.*

Searching for what?

*Or who?*

The thought coiled in her gut like a snake.

Uthru's voice broke the quiet, each word weighted with resignation. 'Then we ask for volunteers. Three, no more. To seek the Seer at Washrock Rise and return with counsel.'

No one moved.

Sparks rose and died, swallowed by night. Someone added wood to the flames—they surged higher, throwing new shadows that danced across frozen faces.

Niama's pulse hammered in her ears. She looked around the circle. Saw fear in every face. Saw parents gripping their children's shoulders. Saw hunters—skilled, brave hunters who'd faced boar and bear—staring at the ground as if answers might rise from the soil.

No one would volunteer. She knew it in the settling silence, in the way eyes found anything to look at except Uthru's face.

Her hands trembled. She clenched them.

The tracks were at the cairn. The place where she'd been found. Where her story began in blood and mystery.

If something was searching—if something was coming south—it was coming for her.

She could feel it in her bones. In the dreams she'd been having. In the way the forest had felt wrong for weeks, watching, waiting.

She thought of the empty bowl she'd seen in a doorway. Of the children with hollow cheeks. Of two days of meat and then starvation.

She thought of whatever had left her bleeding fifteen years ago. Whatever she'd fled into the forest to escape.

Niama stepped forward.

The circle waited, breath held.

She looked at the hunters—at their fear, poorly hidden. At their relief when she moved, when someone else took the burden.

'We will go.' The words carried across the gathering, clean and unyielding.

She turned to Coseo. His eyes were wide, but he nodded once, jaw set.

'I'm with you,' he said, voice only slightly unsteady.

Movement to her left. A younger man stepped forward—Valran. Niama recognized him from the outer settlements, from occasional hunts where their paths had crossed. Lean, perhaps twenty summers, with a bow slung across his back and callused hands that spoke of long hours with the string.

His voice was steady, but his knuckles were white where he gripped his bow. 'I'll go as well.'

Niama studied him. Dark hair pulled back, sharp cheekbones, eyes that held something fierce beneath the surface. Not just courage. Something else. The need to prove himself, perhaps. Or to escape something.

'You're certain?' she asked. 'Washrock Rise isn't a hunt. It's—'

'I know what it is.' He met her gaze without flinching. 'I've hunted beyond the inner trails. Tracked through the deep woods. I won't slow you down.'

She held his eyes a moment longer, searching for hesitation, for the crack that would appear when fear truly settled in.

She found only determination.

'Very well,' Niama said.

Relief rippled through the gathered crowd like wind through wheat. Shoulders sagged. Parents pulled their children closer. The hunters who'd been staring at the ground now looked up, gratitude and shame warring on their faces.

Uthru inclined his head, something like pride and sorrow mixing in his expression. 'Your courage honors you. Washrock Rise is perilous even in calm times. What you face now—' He paused, collecting himself.

He glanced up through the canopy. Stars shone cold and clear between the branches. 'The new moon rises in four nights. The Seer will speak only then. After, he falls silent for another month.'

A month.

Niama's mind raced. The stores would last two weeks, maybe three if they rationed hard enough. Children would starve waiting for another moon. And if the tracks continued to circle closer—

'The journey is four days in good weather,' Uthru continued. 'In winter, through whatever drives the herds away, with whatever makes those tracks—' His voice roughened. 'You must move faster than safe. Faster than wise.'

He looked at each of them in turn—Niama, Coseo, Valran.

'Depart at first light. Move fast. Don't stop unless you must.' His voice caught, just slightly. 'May the light guide your path. And may you return whole.'

The gathering began to break apart, voices rising again, subdued and worried. Parents hurried children toward home. Hunters dispersed in small groups, heads bent together in urgent conversation.

Lhoris pushed through the crowd without a word, his face dark with anger or fear—Niama couldn't tell which.

As people moved past, an older woman touched Niama's arm. Her face was lined with grief, eyes hollow.

'My son went to Washrock Rise seven years ago,' she whispered. 'We never found his body.' Her fingers tightened, trembling. 'Come back, child. Don't make me mourn twice.'

Before Niama could respond, the woman slipped away into the dispersing crowd.

Uthru appeared at Niama's shoulder. 'All three of you—meet me at the heart tree at first light. There are things you must know before you depart.'

Coseo and Valran exchanged glances, then nodded and moved toward the remaining fires where food still waited.

Uthru touched Niama's arm, holding her back as the others left. The firelight carved deep shadows across his face, making him look older than she'd ever seen him.

'Walk with me,' he said quietly.

They moved beyond the circle's edge, into the space between firelight and forest. The feast's noise faded behind them—voices and crackling flames becoming distant, dreamlike.

'You knew,' Niama said. It wasn't a question.

Uthru stopped, his back to the celebration. 'About the cairn? Yes.' His voice was heavy. 'I was there when the hunters found the first tracks. I sent Rolana to announce it publicly because—' He paused. 'Because I couldn't bear to ask you myself.'

'Ask me what?'

'To walk toward danger when I don't know if that danger knows your name.'

The words hung in the cold air between them.

He turned to face her fully. 'Fifteen years ago, we found you bleeding at that cairn. You were dying, Niama. The wounds—' His voice caught. 'No child should have survived them. But you did. And you healed faster than any elf I'd ever seen. Faster than natural, even for our kind.'

Niama's hands clenched. She'd always known there was something different about her. Cuts that closed in days instead of weeks. Bruises that faded overnight. The elders' careful silence when she recovered too quickly.

'The elders recognized what it meant,' Uthru continued quietly. 'That kind of healing—it's a blessing. Old magic from the first peoples, from bloodlines that walked this world before our kingdoms rose.' His eyes searched hers. 'We didn't know where you came from.

Who your people were. But we knew you carried something ancient in your blood.'

'You never told me.'

'We thought it kinder not to.' Something like shame crossed his face. 'You were a child. Traumatized. We gave you a home, a name, a life. Why burden you with questions we couldn't answer?'

Niama's throat tightened. 'And now?'

'Now tracks appear at the cairn where we found you. Now darkness rises and ancient things wake.' His voice roughened. 'I don't know if it means anything. The forest is vast—the tracks could be coincidence. These creatures range everywhere, and the cairn is simply in their path.'

'But you're afraid it's not coincidence.'

'I'm afraid,' he admitted, 'that when old magic walks the world again, it recognizes its own. Your healing—that blessing in your blood—what if the darkness can sense it? What if whatever you fled fifteen years ago is connected to what hunts the forest now?'

The words should have terrified her. Instead, they felt like relief. Like finally naming the shadow she'd felt watching.

'The dreams,' she said. 'I've been having dreams.'

Something like grief crossed Uthru's face. 'I know. Many do, as the darkness grows. But yours—' He paused. 'Are they visions of what's coming? Or memories of what you survived?'

'I don't know,' she whispered. 'Blood. Screaming. Something vast in the dark. I can never tell if I'm remembering or seeing.'

Uthru gripped her shoulders. 'The Seer will know. He's older than this darkness. Older than our kingdoms. If anyone can tell you what you carry in your blood, what you survived, what's coming—it's him.'

'And if my past and this darkness are connected?'

'Then you've survived it before.' His voice turned fierce. 'Whatever left you bleeding at that cairn failed to kill you. Your blood wouldn't let it. That's not weakness, Niama. If darkness comes again—we'll need that strength. We'll need you.'

Silence settled between them. In the distance, someone laughed—a bright sound, incongruous with the weight pressing down on Niama's chest.

'I'm afraid,' Niama admitted.

'Good. Fear keeps you sharp.' He released her, stepped back. 'The Seer may have answers about what's coming. About what hunts the forest. And perhaps—' His voice softened. 'Perhaps he can tell you who you were before we found you. What people gave you that blessing in your blood.'

'I'm not sure I want to know.'

'No,' he said gently. 'But you need to. Whatever's coming, you'll face it better knowing the truth than running from shadows.'

The firelight flickered between the trees, painting everything in uncertain shades.

'First light,' Uthru said. 'Then I'll tell you and the others what I know of Washrock Rise. What to expect. What to fear.' He turned to go, then paused, looking back over his shoulder. 'Niama—your volunteering tonight. That took more courage than the others know. More than you know, perhaps. Thank you.'

Then he was gone, his form swallowed by shadow and smoke, leaving her alone with questions that had lived beneath her skin for fifteen years.

Now they had teeth.

Niama stood in the darkness between fire and forest, listening to the celebration fade behind her. Somewhere in the trees, something watched and waited.

She turned back toward the light, toward the warmth and voices, and tried not to think about how soon she'd be leaving it all behind.

# ABOUT THE AUTHOR

Derren Parsons is the Australian author of the compelling new adult fantasy series, *The Chronicles of Arghost*. Some of his other titles include *The Jonathon Rourke Series, Raven's Bane*, and *The Magika Handbook*. He makes his online home at www.DerrenParsonsAuthor.com. You can connect with Derren on Twitter at @DParsonsAuthor, Facebook at www.facebook.com/AuthorDParsons, Instagram at https://www.instagram.com/derrenparsonsauthor/ and you should send him an email at contact@derrenparsonsauthor.com if the mood strikes you.

# Have you read them all?

## The Magika Handbook

### A Comprehensive guide

The Magika Academy of the Arts Handbook is a vital resource for aspiring Magikas, providing important information on Arghost's flora and its properties. Students must treat the handbook with respect, dedicating time to studying it and internalizing its teachings.

To tap into the unique energy of Arghost's flora, one must embrace introspection, mindfulness, and a willingness to explore the unknown. Each biome on Arghost provides unique opportunities for discovery, but precision and mental acuity are necessary to blend the right plants in the right amounts. Becoming a proficient Magika requires years of focused, dedicated, and disciplined training, and success depends on one's abilities, resolve, and commitment to the craft. The handbook provides a starting point, but the true potential of magic is only limited by imagination and creativity.

**AVAILABLE AT MOST ONLINE RETAILERS**

## The Second Rising

### The Chronicles of Arghost Volume I

The realm of Atheron teeters on the precipice of darkness, as an ancient evil awakens. Thrust into a monumental conflict, Niama, a skilled elven huntress from the Enchanted Erebour Forest, seeks to unravel an arcane prophecy. When a fateful encounter with a mystical seer unveils a foreboding prophecy, Niama embarks on an epic odyssey to recover Athris's lost weapon before insidious forces doom Atheron into darkness.

Joined by Kesaahn, a formidable magika wielding arcane gifts, and Rohan, the valorous prince successor, Niama navigates foreboding realms despoiled by occult forces, battling the merciless darkness while pursuing clarity regarding the prophecy's obscured designs. With the fate of Atheron at stake, the companions undertake a heroic journey to find the mythical Staff of Light and uncover the prophecy's meaning before it's too late.

Wrestling with haunting secrets from her past, Niama races against time, braving treacherous terrain and sinister entities while striving to decipher the remaining riddles. Can her unwavering resolve illuminate the path forward? Or will the darkness extinguish Atheron's radiance forever?

**AVAILABLE AT MOST ONLINE RETAILERS**

## Fate's Wager

### Every Gamble Has Its Price.

When ex-soldier John's gambling debts embroil his family in a treacherous quest, he assembles a fellowship from his dark past—a cunning human, stalwart dwarf, fierce elven huntress, and twin Namites, jackal-headed warriors from a distant desert land. Bound by brotherhood forged through the calamities of war, they dare to pursue fabled treasure stolen by a legendary sea beast.

Braving untold dangers on land and sea, John's eclectic band of battle-hardened rogues must work as one to outwit ruthless brigands and monstrous jungle horrors in their drive to settle John's score. But as deception and betrayal threaten to tear the team apart, only their unwavering camaraderie can conquer the challenges ahead.

In this epic tale brimming with magic, mythic monsters, rip-roaring action, and sprawling world-building, one man's debt holds dire implications, forcing him to lead his team of damaged heroes on a breakneck chase that will either end a lifelong curse... or destroy everything he holds dear.

**AVAILABLE AT MOST ONLINE RETAILERS**